Simeon

KATHI S. BARTON

This is a work of fiction. Names, characters, places, and incidents are products of the author's imagination or are used fictitiously and are not to be construed as real. Any resemblance to actual events, locations, organizations, or persons, living or dead, is entirely coincidental.

World Castle Publishing, LLC
Pensacola, Florida
Copyright © Kathi S. Barton 2018
Paperback ISBN: 9781949812244
eBook ISBN: 9781949812251
First Edition World Castle Publishing, LLC, November 12, 2018
http://www.worldcastlepublishing.com

Licensing Notes

Cover: Karen Fuller
Editor: Maxine Bringenberg

Prologue

Anthony rubbed his head. If this kept up, he was going to need a powder for his pain. He looked at Eve when she sighed heavily. They were getting nowhere fast in this conversation, and he wasn't sure what to do about it. Looking at the woman before him, he tried once more to get her to stand up and come closer. Sometimes being king made things unbearably difficult.

"Brynhilde, I would wish to talk to you secretly. If you stay there, plastered to the floor for the entire time, I'm not going to be able to speak to you properly. Come. Let us speak." She didn't move, not even to look up at him. "Damn it, woman. I'm needing something from you."

"You wish to claim me." He didn't want to. It hadn't been in their plans to do anything like that. To claim her, to make her his servant, would be wrong on so many levels. "My lord, you know what I am and what I do. I cannot, without going against my laws, the ones that you put into place, speak to you where my head is higher than your own. I am but a warrior, not an equal to you or anyone."

"Show yourself." Anthony looked at Eve when she spoke. It was unlike her to be so hard, her voice full of command. "Stand and show yourself, all of yourself, to us. Now, Brynhilde. That way we can judge your worth to us."

The woman stood, and Anthony realized how young she looked. He knew her to be old and powerful, but the appearance of her youth startled him speechless. Not so his lovely mate. She was rarely speechless, not when it mattered the most. And this did, more than anything they'd done thus far.

"You will show us your warrior. Then we'll talk about claiming. If need be we will, but for now, I wish to see what you have to offer." The woman raised her brow but said nothing. Brynhilde wasn't one to fuck with, he knew this. She was as powerful as she was hateful. He was glad that he'd not have to be mated to her. "Where is this supposed warrior that we have heard so much about?"

Her arms stretched above her head. He knew it was for show...or perhaps she had been taught to bring her magic that way and it had stuck with her. But he could see the magic gather around her and stepped back. This was going to be epic, and he was excited for it, but also, if he was honest with himself, a little frightened.

Light danced along her body...sparkled, he supposed. Her hair, dark before, turned a bright red, fiery he thought. And as it lengthened, tangling with her body, wrapping her up, her armor began to show itself. Anthony knew now this was for them, a show of power and force. As her armor strengthened and wrapped around her, wings appeared behind her, as brilliant a green as her eyes, of which nothing of her body showed but that.

She would and could fight an army now, and come out on the other side as the victor. The woman oozed strength, confidence, and magic. He would only want to be on her side. To be on the other would mean that all was lost. Brynhilde was epic.

When her show of force was complete, she flittered above the floor before raising her sword and sticking it deep into the stone floor as she came down in her stance. He would never go by that spot without thinking of her, however little time he had left.

Her chest plate was silver, a hue so bright that it was nearly blinding. There was no crest upon it, and there wouldn't be until she was claimed by another force. As she stood there, her wings spread wide and high, her hair, the massive amount that hadn't become her armor, ever flowing behind her head, Anthony was struck by her beauty. And the scar that went from her left eye to her chin did nothing to take away from that. He stepped forward enough to touch her, but stopped when she raised her sword.

"Do ye claim me as your own?" Anthony had a moment where he was slightly afraid, not of her personally, but of what she'd do to his son once she went to him. His son, and that of Jacob, would know a real kind of devotion should she fall in love with the boys. Or she would slaughter them.

"Brynhilde, where is your family?" He saw the pain there, the flicker of it as it passed over her face. He wanted to tell his Eve to stop, but before he could, she spoke again. "You have no one claiming you...you could have a family. Where are your parents? Sisters and brothers?"

"Dead, my lady." Anthony felt compelled to hold her,

to wrap her up in his arms so that the pain would be his as well. To lessen it for her. "They were killed when I was at war. My master then...my master did not care for me and my rules, so he had them all murdered. I have found all but one of them, the ones that killed my family, and when I find him, he'll suffer like no other for his orders to murder them. He committed a cowardly act by not being there himself, and now he will pay as well."

"I am sorry." Brynhilde looked at him when he spoke softly. "I am truly sorry for all that you have lost. It would hurt me beyond words to have lost all that I love."

He would, and soon, if things were to go as they were foretold to them. As he moved to his seat beside Eve, he took her hand into his. It was well past time they asked of her the favor that would put her with their son and Jacob's.

"There is a book that needs to go to the future king." The wings flittered again, not enough to lift her up this time, but they moved all the same. Anthony continued just as Tinsel, Brynhilde's brownie and companion, came into the room. "There will be a great war, one where you will be hidden away so that you will not have to pledge allegiance against this kingdom. I do this for you so that you can avenge your family when all is done. And it will be over someday, just not in our lifetime."

"You are an immortal, same as me." She dropped her head, asking for forgiveness for pointing out what he already knew. Anthony walked to her then and lifted her face up to his. She was tall, and he could see the fear there in her eyes. "You cannot die, my lord king. I will fight with you."

"'Tis too late for that, I fear." She watched his face, seeing what no other, save his mate, could see there...the future, and

8

what would happen to them. "I need for you to take him this book. His name is Asher, called that from the ash of this castle when it has fallen. Someday the castle will be repaired…the magic that we leave behind will help him rebuild, to make things right again for all who would dwell here. The book and all that it represents will be in your hands."

"And this son…what will he demand from me in return for this favor?" Anthony told her nothing, but that he was going to be as good a king, if not better than him. "I do not believe that, my lord. You are a good and kind man. Your wife too. How can this be?"

"He is part of me. Of us. And his mate is as strong as he will be." Anthony had her attention now, and thought he had to do it now or it would be all for nothing. "This thing I ask of you, it is the final key, the last stone that will be placed in the castle. If you do not wish to help me without me claiming you, then I will understand. I will be disappointed, child, but I will understand."

Eve moved to stand behind the warrior. Her armor was as strong as his own scales, her blood as cold as his. But she could use more, would need more in the coming years, and he did not want her harmed in any way. While he touched her, Eve did the same from behind.

The sharing of their magic only took a second or two, but the transformation to the warrior was profound. She stood there before him, and he knew that she was in a great deal of pain. But as he watched her, nothing moved on her; her eyes did not blink to show that she hurt.

"You have given me too much." He shook his head. Her voice was rough, like even that was in pain. "You have. I can feel it through my body, like blood rushing from an open wound. Why would you do such a thing to me?"

"You will need it, this I promise you. Once you have given the book to Asher, when the castle he rebuilds is nearly complete, you will never have to be claimed again by a man that wishes only for your sword." She nodded and then staggered slightly. "Careful now. You are going to need to hibernate for a while at least."

Touching her armor now, the chest plate that protected her heart, he put his mark upon it. Not that she'd see it, not yet, but it would be there for Simeon and his own child, her mates, to see. To know that she came to them with his blessings.

The other women, some of them already on their path, others not yet born, would come to the men that would be family to him. They'd make them stronger still, love them beyond words, and give them a part of their magic and love that would sustain them forever. But this one, this warrior of the fairies, had been the hardest one to convince.

Her heart would be hardened by the time they came together, his children and her, and sadly, she would hurt more than the others when she came to them. Not with her sword, but it would cut just as deeply and painfully. Stepping back when she seemed to be able to stand on her own two feet, he watched her stretch again, this time trying out her newfound power. After she left them, the book in her hand — to rest, she told him — he sat in his chair and thought of this woman.

"She will be furious in her fighting. And so loving when that is called for too. Of all the women that will come to our yet born children, I think she will be the best of them all." Anthony nodded but said nothing yet to his queen. "You worry overly much. What's done is done for them. There is nothing else we can do but to ready things here for them. We have done more than we should have, love, but they'll be safe now."

"I so wish I could see them." Eve said that she did as well. "There will be children of them. Grandchildren of ours that we will not spoil or touch. It is the saddest thing next to losing you, I think. Not being able to see them grow and become men. Having their own young and playing with them."

"Someday, we'll look down on them and smile. Our children will live. That is all we've ever wanted for them." He agreed; it was all they had thought of since seeing visions of their own deaths. "Anthony, what will become of her? You know, do you not?"

"I do. I am saddened by the things she must do and will do to survive. But she will. And while she'll be stronger for it, it will harden her heart too." He looked at his one true love. "Let us talk of more pleasant things. Take a lunch to the lake and make love there. The babes will be safe for an hour or two."

"Yes, I'd like that very much." He nodded, standing up. "You have talked to Tinsel? He will know what is going on and help her?"

"I will when we return. He will do this, I know, but it will hurt them both that we need him to do this one more thing for us." Eve nodded as they made their way to the kitchen to get some food. "We have gained so much from this, but are losing so much more."

"Yes, but the safety of our children and those of Sally and Jacob will be more than we could have hoped for during this time, don't you think?" He did and told her that. "I love you, my love. More than I could ever be able to tell you. You are my heart, my soul."

~~~

Tinsel came back just as she was burrowing into the ground. Bryn watched him fly around making things right for her before she told him to sit down and be quiet. He did so, but he pouted about it. She asked him where he'd gone.

"I will be here until you have awakened. I wished to gather me some things up. They're in my pocket." He had a magical pocket. He could carry a man in it should it be necessary. Or her, which he had once before. "Do you wish for me to sing to you?"

"No." Clearing her throat, fearful that he would sing anyway, she tried again. "I'm ready to rest now. And your singing might keep me awake. I think the king gave me a bit of something to pull me under faster."

He nodded and looked around them. She wanted him to rest as well, but he would not. And he'd more than likely sing too, once she was asleep. Bryn felt sorry for the creatures around them, ones that could not get away from his noise. Tinsel could not sing.

Words he didn't know he made up, sometimes making the song he sang seem more silly than heartfelt. And he had no tone. Nor could he carry a tune. The man was as deaf to the music he sang as she wished she was when he did it. Closing her eyes, she smiled.

"My lady, when you wake, what is our plan then? Did you have an idea to stay here?" Yawning, she told him that she thought she'd be better off here than anywhere else. "Mayhap. But should you like to travel a bit, that would be good too. We could keep ahead of the men who would want you to fight for them."

"You could be right. I'll speak of it with you when I rise."

Yawning again, she adjusted the rocks that covered her, disturbing the small creatures that had bedded down before her. "Tinsel, you are my one and only friend...you know that, do you not? I have no need for others in my life, save you."

"I thank you for that, my lady. But you have no one else in your life because you have a sword at the ready when anyone gets close. Think of the friends we might have should you not be in competition all the time." She laughed, as did he. "We are good for each other, neither of us needing much. We have all that we can carry because I was gifted a pocket, and when we are fighting, we are stronger than the others and can live for another day."

Living another day did not have as much appeal to her as it did him. When she'd had her family around, a place she could go and be loved, it had been her greatest joy. Now... well, now there wasn't much for her to be happy about. She did her job, and did it well, then rested until someone else found her. There would never be death for her.

Bryn could weaken to the point where she would need to hibernate, but not die. It was what made her so sought after. Wounds that she received in the line of duty—for one king or another—had been so horrendous that she would be down for several months...once a whole year. But death, as had claimed her family, her sisters, and brother, hadn't been her right.

"Is the king aware of what you did to your last master?" Bryn told Tinsel that he more than likely knew. "Yes, you could be right on that. Your.... My lady, if you don't mind me saying so, you were very violent toward him and his men. Not that I blame you...I loved your family as well. But if he had seen only a bit of what I did in the end, he might not have you coming around to.... He might not have wanted your help."

"Nay. Like everyone, he only wants me for my sword, so I will do this. He thinks that I will not; it was there, in his head, that I'd not do this for him. So, I will, just because of that. But a book? How does he think it will be needed to rebuild a castle? I think he only jests me." Sleep was getting harder to fight, so she stopped. "Tinsel, when I wake, we'll go on a grand adventure, you and me. We'll go and see the world."

"Yes, I should like that." His voice sounded so sad that she wanted to ask him what the matter was. But sleep took her, as profoundly as the magic had from the king and queen.

When she woke, Bryn lay very still. She didn't know where she was, what time of the day it was, or what she'd find when she moved out of her hiding place. There were voices... she could hear them, but didn't understand what they were saying. It wasn't until Tinsel spoke that she calmed a little.

"You have been asleep, my lady, for more than a few days." She asked him how long in the same whispered voice that he had used. "A decade. No more than that, I think."

"A decade? You are sure?" He said that he was, very much so. "I don't understand. How was I to rest for that long of time? I was not wounded."

"I know not, my lady warrior, but I was beginning to worry some." He appeared in front of her, his voice still very low. "There are others above us. They fight even now. Should you rise up, there is a chance that one of them will claim you. I think you should not join them. Both of them will want you, and nothing will be solved as they fight for your sword."

"I shall stay here then." He thought that was a good idea. "Tinsel, I have been here for a decade. Yet I feel as if I have only rested but a moment. What did the king do to me?"

14

"As I have said, I know not. But I have some sad news, my lady. He is dead. As is his lady wife." Her heart broke for the couple. While she didn't understand them, she had liked them a little. "The castle is in ruin. The townspeople still fight over the lands left unattended. There is much fighting between neighbors, and even families. It is not a time that we should be in. After all this time, there is no one to rule, and I fear for all."

"The child of the king, has someone saved it?" He said that he hadn't heard of anyone that claimed the child, or any word if it had lived through the fire. "This might be all for naught, Tinsel. Their child might not have lived for me to give this book to. Whatever will happen to him should he be out there?"

"He will come, this I know. The king said that he could see into the future, and he would have seen that his child lived." She nodded and asked about the ability to move out of her place. "Let me check for you. I am glad to have you awake now. I have seen so much. I have even worked on my singing for you. I know a great many tunes now to lull you to rest."

When she was finally free from her sleeping place, she knew that she'd been not just hibernating, but she had been becoming more. She was stronger than ever. Her armor was thicker on her body, and she could hide it with just a thought. Changing her appearance had been easy for her before, but now she only had to think of something and it was changed. There wasn't even a drain on her magic to hold herself in another form. Looking at Tinsel, she asked him what she needed to know. Anything that would keep them from being claimed right away.

"Everything, my lady. The castle is indeed fallen. There

was much fighting and deaths. I have seen so much while you lay in your slumber." She told him she was sorry. "No need for that. You have become more than before, haven't you? And I think that good, for not just you, but for all mankind, should they survive this. It is terrible. But you are well?"

"Yes. The magic of the king and queen together has made me able to rest less, I think. Even my sword is stronger. I can feel my blood rushing over me, making me stronger still. But they are dead. I thought...well, I assumed that when they were killed my magic would go with them." He flew up to her shoulder and sat down. "We should leave this place, Tinsel. I do not want to be caught up in a battle that I know nothing about."

As they made their way through the woods and beyond, all she could think about was the child that had not lived. Just as she was moving toward a home of some worth, she saw the children in the yard and watched them for a bit. They were big boys, all three of them, and she wondered who they belonged to. Turning away to make her way to the next town over, she was seen by another of the boys, this one smaller than the others.

He didn't speak to her, just stared. Realizing that he could only see what she wanted him to—a woman, not the warrior that she was—Bryn moved away from him and the house to find a safer place. But his face, the one that looked up at her with such innocence, made her heart twist up in pain. Her brother had such a look when he'd been alive.

Paul had been her friend and her brother. She'd loved her sisters as well, but they were such little girls, all of them worried for their hair or some such thing. But Paul had been someone that she could talk to, come to when she needed a hug. One that didn't care if she mussed him up with mud or more. Bryn thought that she'd miss him the most. He was the best little boy she'd ever known.

It took them four days to travel to the next village over. There was great strife all over, people wanting to come to the lands and take them over. No one could…there was magic all around the place. But she knew that someday, someone would come and break it down, and she wanted nothing to do with it but handing him the book. If he still lived.

"My lady, how about here?" They were far away from the ruined castle, yet could still see smoke curling from the smaller fires that had been homes of the villagers. Even after all this time, the fires that burnt there had not stopped burning. "I can get us some dinner and we can see about a home for us. Temporary, of course, but it will be nice to rest for a bit. And to have a roof over our heads. It will be better than the stone you laid upon, don't you think?"

Bryn had forgotten that he'd been awake when she wasn't, watching over her so that no one would bother her. He could have awoken her, she knew this, but he hadn't so that she could be ready. Ready for what, she didn't know, but Bryn knew that something or someone would come soon.

"This is fine."

He nodded and set to work finding dinner. While he was gone she thought of a little house, just big enough for the two of them, and was surprised when it started to build for them. The ground moved, the trees felled themselves for the walls. Furniture was built for them, as well as a bed and a table. And when Tinsel returned, she told him what she'd done.

"The magic of the king and queen. It was said that they could work the elements when they needed. They must have passed some along to you. This is good. We'll be safe here for a while." He took the berries into the home and came out smiling. "You might have thought of your empty belly too. There is much in the way of foodstuffs. You have done well, my lady. And I, for one, will enjoy the fresh flowers that are set upon the table for me."

Bryn helped him with the house, moving things around to the way they wanted. She put magic around the place too, to keep others from finding them. She thought she could live here forever when they settled in the bed that night, but knew that she'd not be able to. Bryn needed to keep moving or else she would be captured. And as much as she wanted to use her new powers, her new sword too, she wasn't ready to shed any more blood just yet. There had been enough of it for years to come, she thought.

The next morning, she was in the kitchen having some tea when her little friend came by to see her. He was commenting on the lovely home when she remembered something. Turning to him, she asked.

"Tinsel, you have the book still." He patted his pocket. "Good. We'll set up a plan, a pack to grab when we need to move, and we'll keep atop it too, so that we never lose it. Should we do that, I don't know what will happen to the world ahead. I think we should load your pocket too. With foodstuff that cannot spoil. A few wraps for bandages as well. Not too heavy for you, but enough to get us started if we have to go quickly."

"I will hold it all, my lady. And keep it safe. This is a good plan. I shall work on some meat to dry, as well as some herbs for our sup should we run." He sounded so sure that she wanted to ask him why he was. Tinsel wasn't ever sure about anything. Even if rain was falling upon his head while he stood there, he would doubt his own mind. "Shall I make us a meal?"

As before, she let it go. Bryn might well talk to him later about it, but for now her belly was growling at its emptiness, and she wanted to look around. With so much going on, there was a quiet that made her nervous. She did wonder, too, when the castle would be rebuilt. She wanted to get this over with for the king.

They talked for a long while, him telling her what he'd seen, how he'd kept her safe. She was sure that some of it was less than what he said, but she didn't mind. Bryn doubted greatly that he'd slayed an army of men in her absence, as well as caught large fish with his bare hands. But she loved this little man, and he had kept her safe. She just hoped that she could keep him equally as safe in the coming years.

Chapter 1

"No, no, no. That just won't work for me. You should just call my sister and tell her that she needs to come here and take care of this. I have friends that would do it, but they're all very busy right now." Cora looked around the courtroom. No one was there that she knew. Even her family, William and her sons, weren't there to be with her. "Judge, you really are doing this all wrong. I'm surprised that you've made it this far with your bumbling around about things. Listen to me tell you once again how it should be going."

"Am I? My having a college education, passing my bar, and even doing this every day for the last thirty some odd years makes me believe I'm more qualified to decide how this should go than you are. And even if you think I'm not, then you'll have to deal with your consequences. Your sentencing is before you, Ms. Daniels. You'll be taken to jail as early as tomorrow morning." She didn't want to go to jail. It was beneath her and her status. But no one would listen to her. "As for your sister taking care of this for you? Even should she have offered, which she did not, I wouldn't allow her to pay for your trouble. You make it yourself, and the fact that you think that someone else should be responsible for your crimes is beyond me."

"Why not? I mean, she has it. It's not like she has any idea how to be rich. Besides, I've got things to do. It's almost Christmas, and I have a lot of friends and family to purchase for. My goodness, this is going to be a nightmare if I don't have my annual party. People come from other states just to have a bit of my ham and glazes. And the gifts that I give out are legendary. You have to see that you're holding me here against my will. How am I expected to get anything done about the holidays if you won't just let me go?" He just laughed a little. "You think this is a joke? I have been here for nearly a month now, and you've yet to let me have my cell phone or my own clothing. Not to mention, that nasty food has to be improved for the next person."

"Has anyone ever pointed out to you that you're a very demanding person? That you twist things up so that they benefit only you? You've been a pain in the bottom for that entire month too. The station where you're being held is going to go on strike should I return you there. I'm sure that even your ex-husband might have said that once or twice to you." She told him that William was her husband and that he'd never do that. "Then he's better off without you, I'm thinking. You will be remanded to the state penitentiary at nine in the morning. You will serve a sentence of no less than four years. And in that time, you will work off your debt to the credit cards, as well as pay for court costs. There is also—"

"When will I get them back?" He asked her what. "The credit cards. If I must pay them off, then I should have them returned to me. I told you, several times, I have things to purchase from my cell, since you can't get your head out of your bottom and let me out for anything like shopping. And since you're making me go to the jail, which is not the way things should have gone, then I'll need a computer as well as Internet service. Also, my cell phone. I don't like using the one in the hallway back there. Everyone can hear me. And I want my clothing. I hate those suit things. I have a list of things that need to change too. How do you expect someone of my standing to eat that slop that they're serving me? And when I asked for a salad, I was given unwashed lettuce with nothing but a boiled egg on it. It was disgusting. I had to toss the entire meal away, I was so put off."

He just stared at her. Cora knew that he was in awe of her. Few would stand up for their rights, and he was impressed by her. Or at least she hoped so. There was so much riding on him giving her what she wanted. William wouldn't have the first idea what to get the boys for Christmas, and she'd end up with some stupid sweater or something that she'd have to return. It was better for everyone if she just bought her own gift and put his name on it. And he'd not save the receipts for anything either. The way things were going, the local charity place was going to get a lot of unused things after she got home. William had to know that she had standards, and he'd never get them right.

"Ms. Daniels, you are in jail for credit card debt, credit card fraud, credit card theft, as well as a plethora of other things. Why on earth would you think that anyone, even me, would hand over credit cards to you again? You are in debt, as you have willingly admitted you did, for well over six hundred thousand dollars' worth of charges, back payments, interest, and penalties." She waited for him to tell her how she was going to use them if he wasn't cooperating when he shook his head at her. "You are by far the most stubborn woman I've ever had the unpleasantness of having in my courtroom. There is no way you're going to get any of those things. And it's doubtful that anyone in their right mind would even give you a card after this. If they do, then heaven help them because I doubt you'd have any intention of paying a single one of them back. I'm done. Court is adjourned."

When she was jerked up from her seat, she tried to pull away. The police officer that held her arm was much stronger than she looked, and Cora had to follow along with her or be dragged across the floor. This was an outrage. She, of all people, shouldn't be treated this way. But as they took her back to the van she had arrived here in, she glared at the officer. Cora hated everyone at this moment.

"I want to call my sister, Gracie. She has to take care of this for me." The officer said nothing as she sat there, smiling at her. "Are you stupid as well as ugly? I want a phone to call Gracie. I don't like her, but she sure as hell can get me out of this mess that she put me in. All she had to do was what I told her and this would be over. But no, she had to be stubborn. But I won't put up with it any longer. She owes me."

"How do you figure she owes you anything?" Cora didn't know, but it wasn't really any of her business. "'Sides, she's not been in to see you much after you had that tell all with her. She's having a good life, married to a good man who takes good care of her. You did this all on your own."

"Gracie hasn't found anyone to love her. She's just saying that to make me mad." Why she'd do that wasn't anything that Cora had thought through, but it would be like her to tell

24

lies just to get back at her. Gracie was always jealous of her, and the fact that she thought she had to lie to these people too showed how desperate she was about her life looking as good as Cora's. "I'm the one that made a good choice in marriage. She married that *artist* that got himself killed with her baby. Stupid twit had nothing, and she has less now."

"Yet you sit there and tell me that she has to take care of this for you. You gotta make up your mind, girly. Either she is well off, which she is, or she's a twit that has nothing. I've been to her house. You should see it. Beautiful, and decorated with the finest things." Cora told her she lied. "Nope. And her new family? They got more money than all the richest people in the world combined. But they don't flaunt it, nor lord it over others that don't have as much. You should take a few lessons from her. Oh, and your momma? Well, not a nicer person in the world than her. She is teaching first grade at the local school."

"My mother is not teaching anyone. She's too lazy. Not to mention, I don't think she's smart enough to teach herself, much less a room full of kids." Her mom had been a teacher before. Before Father had died and her and Gracie had come along. "Why must you make these things up when you know I can ask them when they come to see me? It's like you've taken lessons in being cruel. Is that it? You're using your new skills on me? I don't like it. Nor you."

"You'll see that I don't care if you like me or not. So, there you go. And if they come to see you, you go right on ahead and ask them. Not that I think you're going to get much of an opportunity. What with you going to the big house in the morning." She laughed again. "Yes, ma'am. I'm not going to miss you one little bit. And you'll be having so much more fun up there too." There was that.

Cora didn't want to go anywhere. Not that she wanted to stay here, but going further away meant that no one would come to see her. And so far, all she'd had as visitors had been the police and the four walls. As much as she hated to admit it, Cora was slightly afraid they'd all forgotten how much they needed her.

"Looks like you got some company." She looked where the officer was and saw someone there. It took her a few moments to figure out who it was. The officer leaned in and whispered it was her mom.

Her mother was standing in front of the jail looking as lovely as she'd ever seen her. Of course, Cora would have looked better, but her mom was pretty today. Not that she'd tell her that. Cora knew that she'd be able to find flaws as soon as she was up close to her. Getting out of the van and being taken into the building, she was pissed off that she couldn't speak to her mother before she had to change back into her clothing that she hated, as well as being checked again. Cora thought they got a perverse thrill out of body checking her every time she had to go to court. Where did they think she was going to get something? They never left her. Or where she was supposed to stash something anyway was beyond her. But they did it, every single time.

"It's not like someone wasn't with me every step of the way there and back. Where do you think I would have gotten anything you might be looking for?" No answer, but then she'd come to expect that. "Damn it, my mother is here. Can't you just hurry this along?"

Once she was dressed in the orange jumpsuit that she hated more than she did the way her hair was now, Cora sat in the chair with a chain on her wrists. She was so mad it made her head hurt. When her mother was shown in and seated, Cora felt her temper go off the charts. There wasn't a single flaw about her mother.

"You look like a hooker, Mother. The color is all wrong for you, and the blouse makes you look like you've put on about fifty pounds." Mother only smiled. "Who picked those things out for you, Mother? Gracie, I bet. She never had any taste in clothing either. Once I get out of here, we'll go shopping. And since I've been denied my credit cards, you'll have to pay for it. But I know all the best places. Places that won't make you look like a streetwalker."

"Really? Because you think what you're wearing is so much better? And for your information, I love what I'm wearing. I have lots of things I love now. As for going shopping, we both know that's not going to happen anytime soon, Cora. You'll be in prison for a long time." That hurt, but she only smiled at her. "I heard that you're going away tomorrow. I wanted to come tell you goodbye, and to tell you that I won't be visiting you. Neither will the boys."

"You're keeping them from me?" She said that they didn't want to see her. "Who's been telling them things about me? You? Gracie? I won't have it, Mother. They're my boys, and I won't have it. You make them come here. I want to hear what you've been telling them to try and turn them against me. You won't do it, no matter what plans you have up your sleeve. I want them here."

"Well, that's just too bad for you. I'm glad you've given up the notion that you're having another child. All the trouble that you caused with that…well, it turned out well for us. To think that you were lying to everyone about something so precious as having another man's child." Cora said nothing. If she did, there would be consequences. The courts had told her that she was sane, and that if she mentioned the nonexistent baby again, she would be in bigger trouble. "Anyway, I was in town and figured I'd come to see you before you left. You have a good life. I'm sure that if you were sunning on a beach somewhere, you'd find fault with it, so I'm going to say my goodbyes."

"When is Gracie going to come here? I have a few things I want her to clear up for me. She shouldn't have left me here this long as it is. I can't purchase things for my children for Christmas." Mother said nothing but only sat there. "Also, I want her to talk to someone about me getting a better living arrangement. I've been stuck here, for no reason, long enough, and I want to get my home back. This is not how someone like me is to spend their life. Gracie needs to get herself here and make sure that I'm out in time for the holidays. It's the least she can do for me."

"You're talking in circles, Cora. No one is going to pay for your problems. You're not leaving here until you've paid things back, and you don't have a home. Not that you'd ever made that place a home. It was a showcase that you filled with things you didn't own and no one liked. You've fucked up, and now you're paying the price for your stupidity." Her mother had never had the nerve to speak to her like this, and Cora wasn't happy about it. But before she could tell her to shut up, she continued as she stood up. "You're the worst daughter I've ever known, Cora. You're selfish and mean. You expect everyone to do your bidding, and you're ungrateful as well. I'm glad that you're here. A place where I hope you learn how to become a better person."

After her mother left and Cora was taken back to her cell, she thought of all the things she wished she'd said to her. Well, she did think she was being polite in not telling her mother a few things too. But Cora wasn't like that. Nor was she what her mother had said. And she never would be either.

"Selfish and mean? I don't think so. I'm just a person who likes things to be perfect. It's not my fault that no one knows how to do anything as well as me." She glared at the toilet and the sink that she had. "I hate how these people have reduced me to be a commoner. I'm going to get out if it's the last thing I ever do. Then I'll show them."

~~~

Bryn opened her eyes and knew she wasn't alone in the barn. It had been a few days, this she knew, but how many she wasn't entirely sure. As she laid there, holding onto herself so that she'd not alert the person with her, she heard a male's laughter. Pissed off, she pushed her way to the top of the heap of hay and shifted at the same time. She knew her mistake the moment that she saw the two men with her.

"Brynhilde, I presume." She nodded, unable to not answer him, his powerful voice showing her that he was her superior in most ways. "I claim you."

He stood up then, and she found herself on her knees before him, her armor covering her from throat to hips. As she waited for him to finish the claiming, the second man stood up. Neither of them seemed to know what they were doing, and she was confused more than ever.

"What now?" It wasn't her job to tell them what they had to do to claim her, so she waited on them. "All right then. We want you to go to the land near here and kill the dragons. There are a few there...we're not sure how many, but we want them all dead. As soon as possible."

"Kill the dragons?" The second man nodded, but didn't move to put his crest upon her armor. "I cannot kill them. No one is to kill them, and I especially cannot."

"Why the fuck not?" She told him there were laws, rules that governed her and what she did for others. "So, we've been sitting here, waiting for you to take your fucking nap, for nothing? That isn't really going to work for us; you know that, don't you?"

"I have rules too. There are a great many of them." He sat down, and so did the second man. "Have you ever claimed a faerie before?"

"Faerie? We were told that you were a warrior. That all we had to do was claim you and you'd have to do what we wanted. What else is there to it?" She said nothing again. "Come on, bitch, we don't have all fucking day."

"I cannot give you answers to those questions." She saw Tinsel then, hovering just above the men and behind them. "You must have read them if you knew what I was."

"I didn't. We were told to come here, claim you, and order you to kill the dragons. And witches too." He'd not mentioned witches before, so she didn't either. "Now you're telling me that there are rules we have to follow, and that you can't even kill anything we want you to?"

Bryn reached out to Tinsel when the man jerked her from the floor. It was all it took. She belonged to him now. Her body burned with his desires to murder. Every thought he had, it was now hers. And when he dropped her to the floor, the hay beneath her burned with the power of his needs.

"What the fuck?"

She felt her armor thicken. Her hair began to reach out,

stretch, and wrap around her. It would serve as an extra bit of magic, reaching out to things, the earth or trees, to help her heal and strengthen herself. Both men backed up, their mouths hanging open when she rose, her body ready for whatever they needed of her.

"I am here to serve you and none other." She bowed before them, having no choice now but to do their bidding. Except that she could not kill the dragons. Her sword was now theirs, yes, but she could no more kill the dragons than she could herself. "Might I have the name of my master?"

"Are you fucking kidding me right now? You belong to me?" She didn't answer him…there wasn't any need to, she supposed. Tinsel flew to her, hiding himself inside of her breast plate. "I'm Huston. This is Doug. Holy shit. We have her."

Bryn wanted to stand, take out her sword, and murder them both. She would be justified, she thought…their minds were as sick as she'd ever seen. The dragons, safe from her, were not the only ones that they wanted dead. The list, extensive in what they wanted, was as long as the day was, as her mother used to say. But not only that, they wanted them to suffer, suffer in ways that even she was sickened by.

"We want you to kill all the dragons you find." She told him, again, that she couldn't kill them. "But you said you served me. That's what I want. What we all want, for them to be dead and no longer taking all the resources from the earth."

"They give to the earth, not take." He hit her. Not that it was painful nor very strong, but she felt her armor wrap tighter around her, and she felt Tinsel's anger as well as her own. "I beg your forgiveness, master. But there are rules that—"

"Keep that in mind the next time you tell me no." Saying nothing, she waited for him to continue. "Why can't you kill the dragons? I want a truthful answer, too."

"They were the first paranormals to roam the earth, giving life to the soil, air, and the plants. To kill them would destroy everything that you hold dear." He hit her again, laughing like this was a game to him. "I cannot lie to you. That is the truth."

"I want them dead. All of them. And if you can't do that, then I want you to kill anything and everything that helps them." Again, she could have explained to him that he was a part of the cycle that made the dragons live, but said nothing. "There is a land not far from here. There are people there, the Bensons, who have been gathering them dragons together and helping them. Destroy them."

"Magical grounds?" He told her that no one could enter the area, nor could they see beyond the trees. Bryn knew the land. She herself had come from a part of it.

"You'll go there, kill them all, and bring their.... You'll bring their hearts back to me. I want them on a golden platter."

He poked his friend in the belly, a gesture that she'd seen many times, but understood it no less now than she had before. She thought it indicated that it was funny. But none of this was.

Bryn stood up, ready to do what she was able to do for him, when something occurred to her. The Bensons...they were the very people that she was to go to. Or at least one of them. She could no more kill the family than she could the dragons. Asher, he was the dragon king, and would be the only person in the world, even claimed as she was, that could order her death or for her to no longer be claimed by these men. Then she thought of something. A way to get out of being a warrior to any man, claimed again, and to not have to go through with the wishes of this man.

"Where are you going?" Bryn put her sword at her back. Her other armor, just as lethal as her blade, was there for the taking should she need it. Turning, she looked at the man, then put out her hands and let her magic show him what she had been asked to do. The magic stirred around until a dragon, long dead, appeared before him, then a scroll that she held out to him. "What is that?"

"Our contract." There wasn't any such thing. She only had to be touched to be claimed by the king. Or for him to order her to stand down. But she thought of keeping these men busy while she decided what she had to do. "You must read this over and agree to it. For your safety."

"Safety?" Bryn watched the men, but she did hear Tinsel laugh. "What would come to harm us, with you at our side?"

Bryn could have told him that they'd only ordered her to kill the dragons and those that were helping them. She also could have told them that if they were hurt, a sword drawn against them, they'd die while she would not. But she said nothing, only shoved the "contract" at them while her mind worked.

"When you have finished, you only need to call me. I will be there as soon as possible, wherever you may be." Backing from them, she decided that if the current king was as stupid as these two, she might be able to get out of both the claiming of these two and helping the king with his castle. If there was one. "I must go and prepare."

As soon as they were away, she shifted. She could turn

into anything…hide in plain sight too. So, she shifted to a hawk and Tinsel joined her in the air. They had lied to a master. Or she had. She would suffer greatly for it, for a long while too if not forever, but there was something so incredibly wrong with them. Not just the fact that they wished to kill all dragons, but their minds were filled with jumbled thoughts that were better left unsaid or known.

The mother of Doug, for one. A woman of high moral standards and religious beliefs. She'd set rules for her children, and Doug thought himself above them. Better than her. He wanted her dead, out of his life, so that he could do as he wished without her hanging over his shoulders. And not just dead, but to suffer, suffer as he thought he had when living with her. And when she'd found out about his plan, she did the only thing she could and left them. That or die. And she preferred to live a bit longer.

That was not the way to treat the woman who gave him life…and Huston had planned to help Doug. The sick depravity of their minds was going to hurt a great many people if they found someone to help them. Her for example. She would do as they said to her, with the exception of killing the Bensons or the dragons. Many would die at her hand if they made her.

"My lady, we have done a wrong. We'll pay." She told him that she would be the only one that would pay. "But I am your servant. I should have warned you that you told untruths."

"I know what I said, Tinsel. I'll be the one taking full responsibility. But we must hurry to the dragon king. The book will be his, then I shall tell him of their plans. Not that he might not know them as well, but we must hurry before they summon me again." The property was just ahead. "You must wait here. I do not want you harmed in any way."

He, of course, refused, and she stopped to land on a branch. He was pushing her to hurry to the king. Insisting on it like he hadn't ever done before. It was then, right at that moment, that she knew he knew something. Touching his mind, she stared at him…he did know much more than she did about any of this. She knew that he had only done what the king had told him, but it hurt her more than she could say that he'd betrayed her this way.

"You knew about my life. The way things would go for me. What I was to encounter when I went to the new king." He nodded, then bowed before her. "You knew what my life was going to be, yet, as my friend, you said nothing to me about it. About the mate and the life I would lead? All of it?"

She knew the truth of his knowledge. How the king had summoned him to come back to him. The stories that he'd told him. Bryn had never bothered to look before. She wished now that she had when she first woke. All of it was so that she would be the mate to some person, a person that the king, her king, deemed for her and only her.

"Not all, but I knew that you'd be hardened by the life. You would then find love in the end that would sustain you forever." She said nothing to him, waiting for him to finish. "He forbade me to tell you, my lady. He said that you knowing would change the outcome of yours and his son's lives. I wasn't able to tell you."

"You mean that he was concerned that his son got all that he needed." Tinsel wisely said nothing. "I'm disappointed in you. Very much so. All this time, you could have said something. Even after he was dead, the king, you could have told me what I was to do for him. Is the book even a real thing? Or is this something else that you didn't tell me about?"

"Yes. It is real. There are spells in it that would help the young king. Also with your help, I'm afraid." She looked beyond where they were, to the smoke curling from the chimneys just over the treetops. "You must take it to him. He will be needing it soon."

Shifting to her true self, Bryn leapt to the ground below her. Tinsel followed her, his small body stiff with the unknown. And hurt...she would imagine that he hurt too. But she hardened herself more against it. She no longer trusted her feelings.

He'd not told her, letting her go on with her life as if it had meaning. That she was needed in order for the new king to live and save the dragons. But it, like a great many things, had been thrust upon her. And now she'd been betrayed by the one person that she had trusted like no other.

"I quit you, Tinsel." She turned and looked at him, and could see the hurt and shock on his face. "You have sentenced me to a lifetime of servitude as a prisoner to a man that I do not want. I am never going to be free again. You should have told me. I could have...I don't know what I could have done now. It is far too late. Let me have the book. I shall take it to him now."

As she walked away, leaving him there, she felt her heart break. Her friend, her only true friend, had betrayed her. And for what? A dead king and queen? It hurt her to her core to know that she had never had his honesty.

Chapter 2

Simeon and Akassa weren't sleeping well. Neither of them had had a good night's sleep since Tinsel had come to tell them that their mate was close. He'd not tell them much about her, other than she was a beauty beyond compare and that she had a temper to match such a fiery red head, but nothing about her magical power, nor what she could bring to them.

Simeon looked at Asher when he came to the castle clearing where they were.

"Tinsel is here." Simeon dropped the shovel he was using to smooth out the walkway they were going to cover in small bits of stone that had been set aside for just this purpose. "He said that she has left him and that he no longer is her companion."

"Did he say what happened?" Asher nodded, looking as grim as he'd ever seen him. "Something has happened and you don't want to tell me."

"Yes. I mean, no." Clear as mud as usual. "He's here to

tell us that he no longer is her sidekick. He said he was no longer her backside, but I took that to mean that he no longer worked for her. Have you noticed that he gets his words messed up at times when he's nervous?"

"You mean like you prattle on when you are?" Asher grinned. "What else did he have to say, Asher? You know as well as I that there is more to this than just her quitting her brownie. Tell me so that we can fix whatever it is."

"She's been claimed." He knew what that meant. Someone, a person who needed her services, had come to make claim on her sword. "This person wants her to come here and kill us, and all the dragons. He said that there was more in their minds, these two men that found her, but she doesn't want to do them. Killing the mother of one of them is one example, but Tinsel said that she'd have to do it if he ordered her to. There's something about a contract she gave to them to read over so that she could buy more time."

"Christ." Asher nodded and sat down just as Akassa joined them. Simeon caught him up on what Asher had said. "So, she's close now and has been found. I'm assuming that these people that have claimed her, they are a part of the dragon slayer group that we've been dealing with all along."

"I would think that is a safe bet. Tinsel said that they were young. I don't really know what that means since he's older than we are. They could be in their nineties as far as that goes." Asher looked up just as the little brownie joined them. He was as flat as a piece of paper on the ground, as well as unmoving as the castle was right now. "You may rise, Tinsel."

"I cannot, my lord king." Simeon snickered. He did that every time someone called one of them lord. It pissed Asher off, so that was an added bonus. "I am but a lowly brownie.

Not even one with my own master. She has.... She has, and rightly so, quit me. I have injured her greatly. By farcing untruths, she has left me to my own."

"Fabricating. You fabricated…never mind. Where is she now?" He told Asher that she was on her way here. "I'm assuming that since this other person has claimed her, we should expect the worse?"

"Nay. She has given them a falseness as well. A contract to keep them busy so that she might bring you the book and get away. I think she is planning to leave. That will mean that she will be encased in a prison." Simeon asked him what he meant. "Jailed, I think you call it."

"Incarcerated. You mean that because she lied to this man, she will be punished? Even though it will save the dragons? And the king?" Tinsel looked up at him, then back to the dirt. "I'm not the king, nor am I anyone to be afraid of. Stand and speak to me."

"You're the mate. One of them, at least." Simeon didn't know who had told him, but he figured it was easy enough to figure out since he was the last one. "She's afraid of you, that you'll put her in chains no different than a man who would claim her sword. She would rather face incarcerated than to be with a man who would make demands on her body rather than her ability."

"I'd never do that." Tinsel said that the king had told him that. He glanced at Asher, who only shook his head. "He said that you were all going to be great men. Each of you, special in the magic that you brought to the family. But you and your other half, he told me, would bring everything to fruition."

"What does that mean?" Tinsel said that he didn't know, as the former king had told him only that. "This book…what does it have to do with me?"

"Everything." Simeon didn't know what that meant either, but he was more afraid of that one word than he had been anything else in his long life. Akassa asked him when she was coming here. "Today. As I said, she is on her way here. I know that she must hurry so that the other men do not call to her first."

"She plans to disobey them. Will it be hard on her? This thing that she plans to do?" Tinsel told Akassa that it would be harder than healing from any wound that she had ever had. "Can we call her here?"

"Nay, not you." He glanced at Asher, then back to the ground. "There is only one being that can command her to do her job or not."

The wording of it, the way he glanced again at Asher, had him thinking that he was putting something out there that he couldn't tell them. But Akassa got it and laughed.

"You have to summon her here, Asher. As the king, then command her to not do as these men order her to do. Sort of claim her yourself, I'm guessing." Tinsel smiled at them all and lowered his head again. "Call her. Let's see what we can work out for her."

Asher stood up and looked around. It was one thing, he knew, to call others to you, but to call in a stranger, one that was there to murder you and all you stood for, was something else altogether. Simeon looked at him. There was a question there, one he wasn't sure of. When Asher spoke, Simeon stood up as well.

"I think it should be you. Not to call her to you as I would, on a command, but as your mate. She knows about you, so you call her." Simeon said he wasn't sure that was a good idea either. "Then if it doesn't work, I'll do it. But if you ask and she comes, it might go better for us all. To be honest, I'm not sure what will happen, but I have a feeling that it's going to be difficult no matter who does the calling."

Simeon nodded, then looked at Akassa. "We do this. Together. We'll call her here, if she pleases. If not...well, then we'll go with plan b. Whatever that might bring us."

They stood side by side, and then Akassa spoke. "We ask her like this, I think. Brynhilde Scott, heart of our soul, come to us please so that we might speak." Simeon agreed and they said it. Before the last word was complete, she was standing in front of them. Or a better description would have been, she was ready to kill them both while standing in front of them.

Her armor was...well, he had to say it, it was beautiful. New looking, though he was sure it was older than any of them. Her hair flew behind her. There wasn't a wind anywhere, so he assumed it was her magic. And that Simeon could almost taste it, she was so strong. Her sword, as stunning as her, was drawn and at the ready.

"Who are you?" Simeon introduced himself, then Akassa. Just their names so as not to upset her more. "And you summoned me here...why?"

"To talk. About the book." It was suddenly in his hands. He was sure that she didn't move, not even to blink. "Okay. But you gave it to me, not Asher."

The sword lowered, but she looked no less ready to do them harm. When it disappeared at her back, Simeon assumed that she'd put it in a scabbard there. He wondered what other weapons she might have on her person. Then Asher cleared his throat, and she turned and looked at him. Studied him, he supposed. Turning toward him, she bowed low, then went to her knees. Simeon had a moment of fear that she was going to kill him when she pulled her sword from her back, quite literally from her back, and handed it out to his brother.

"I give myself to thee. I have dishonored your rules. I would only ask that you spare Tinsel. He had no part in my deception of the men who even now call for me." Asher asked if she was in pain. "Pain? I don't understand."

"The men that call for you, the ones that claimed you... does them calling out for you cause you any kind of pain?" She glanced up at Asher, and Simeon could see the confusion on her face. He wondered if anyone had ever asked her about pain before. "How do I make it so that you are no longer claimed by them so that it doesn't hurt anymore?"

"Why?" It was a good question. Asher looked at him and Akassa. It was time to confess, he supposed. Or do whatever it was to let her know that they were her mates.

"You are our mate." She stood up, her sword pointed at his throat. He didn't move, not even to push it away. He could have, he supposed. Or had Asher order her to do it, but he only stared at her. "Do you wish me dead?"

"Yes." He saw the confusion again, then she shook her head. "I don't want to be claimed by any man. Nor two. I have been shackled to someone nearly all my lifetime. I wish only to be free."

"Then you are." She frowned, the point of the blade shaking just enough to cut a small nick into his flesh. "I free you from the bonds of our coming together. Akassa? What say you?"

"Yes, you're free to do as you please. As your mate, one of your mates, I free you willingly to love us or not." The sword lowered, and she stood there. Simeon waited for her to do something, say anything, as she seemed to be lost in thought.

"What sort of trickery is this?" He told her none as he wiped the blood from his neck. "You wish to entrap me. Or to make me do something that I don't want. I'm not stupid."

"No, and I doubt very much anyone would think you stupid. I haven't any idea how old you are—older than me, I think—so you'd have to be smart to have been able to survive." She told him she was an immortal, same as him. "No. You cannot be killed. Removing my head or piercing my heart will end my life. While it will be very difficult to do, it isn't impossible. I think a man would have to be incredibly stupid to approach you with their sword drawn. You'd have them dead before the thought moved through their head."

"I don't care for your logic. You make me sound as if I'm a monster." He told her he was sorry. "I don't understand you. You're not.... What are you playing at?"

"Playing? I'm not. But here, before we talk, if you wish to speak with us, then you should give this to Asher. I'm not sure what is supposed to happen with it, but I think this was your task, to give the book to the new king." She took the book from him and handed it to Asher. "Thank you."

Asher opened the book and thumbed through it. There wasn't much too it...a leather-bound book that had no title on the front of it, nor did it have any kind of special tassels, as the other books did. The ones that had been brought to them, or found when the dead came to request they be found, had been carved on. Some of them looked like they'd been taken to a crafting class and had been the model for all the things there. This one, the one from the king so long ago, was as plain as a brown paper bag.

"There are no words." Asher looked at Simeon as he

thumbed through the book again. "There isn't anything written here. It's just blank pages. Are you sure this is the right book?"

"It is, my lord." Tinsel came forward as he spoke. "The magic must be released before you can see the words written there. Then the castle, his lordship told me, would be complete. He made me repeat it several times to him that night. There are times when I mess up things."

That was very true. He'd messed up things a half dozen times in the few minutes he'd been with them today. Asher sat down when the rest of them did, and he noticed that Bryn sat lower, her head bowed slightly.

"What sort of magic, Tinsel?" Bryn looked at Asher, then bowed again. "I know nothing of the book, save I was to bring it to you when the time was right. When the castle was nearly finished so that it would be helpful in keeping you all safe."

"There isn't anything we can do about it now, so let's go to the house and have dinner." Simeon put out his arm, as courtly as he could remember doing for his mom. "Would you join us, Bryn?"

~~~

Sally enjoyed having all the family at the dinner table. But tonight, this first night, was very special. They were all there…all of her sons were with their mates. Yes, Bryn wasn't a part of it yet, holding herself off a bit stiffly, but she was there and that was all that mattered for now. Passing the last of her potatoes around, she smiled at the woman.

"I remember you. Not well, I'm afraid, but I had seen you around the castle a few times." Bryn nodded, unsure of herself, poor little thing. "I was so sorry to hear about your mother, child. And your family. They were good people. Your father was a good farmer, and he took very good care of you and yours. I was heartbroken when I heard that they'd been murdered."

"My mother knew you as well. She thought you a very wonderful person. And she said that you made the most pleasing sour apple pie." Sally brimmed with the compliment. "They didn't deserve to die like they did."

"No one does. And to have.... Well, we heard that they'd been asleep in their beds when they were attacked. You were away." Bryn nodded, and said that she'd been a servant then too. "Do you know what happened? I'm sorry, but I know very little about your kind. I thought they'd all be fighters like you."

"No, just me. There is a warrior born every ten generations. When I was born, my parents were so terrified that I'd be called upon at an early age. They kept me hidden away as best they could." Sally asked her if she wanted to talk about it, that she'd not meant to hurt her. "It's all right, mistress. It's been a great many years, and while I miss them very much, the hurt isn't as raw. I thank you for asking after them."

"The king, Anthony, he knew what you were?" Bryn nodded at Jacob when he asked. "He was a brilliant man. A good leader. He, too, was murdered, and the more I find out about that night, the more I wish I could have done more to help him and his lady wife."

"He was a good leader. Tricky, but a good man. The night that I was brought to him, I know that I was frustrating him something terrible. He wanted me to stand, talk to him as if I were equal to him. My heart was broken then…my parents and family had only been killed the month before. But he told me that I was to come here and give the book to one called

Asher, so that he could complete the task of the castle rebuild. As you can imagine, I hadn't any idea what he spoke of. The castle that I was in, it stood strong and steady. But he also told me that I was to hibernate. It's what I do when I'm injured badly. He didn't want me to be caught up in the fighting that would go on when the castle fell." Sally watched the boys, Bryn's mates, as she told her tale. "The castle fell while I rested. And when I woke, the smoke still burned in the fallen castle, and fighting men and women, who would otherwise have been friends, still fought over even scraps of food and water rights."

They didn't touch her, as the others did their mates. No holding of her hand. They were already in love with her, she could see that, but they were standing back, waiting for her to trust them. Sally knew that there was little love or trust in the girl's heart. She'd seen too much, been abused more than most. Sally was proud of her children in that moment, more so than she thought she'd ever been.

"How long were you resting? I would imagine that the magic that you received from the king and queen would have been powerful. It was when they zapped me." Bryn looked at Ariannona and frowned as the other woman continued. "Yes, I'm a witch. I knew the king and queen as well."

"You were but a child when I saw you there." Ariannona nodded. "There were others as well. They were witches too. Few of them good, white witches. The black, I think one of them was the cause to it all, but I cannot be sure."

"Yes. Helenia was there, the black witch. She was Essie's mother, but we dispatched her, and a few others along the way. It's been necessary to keep everyone here safe. The dragons, they're our only hope for the future." Bryn frowned again, and looked down as Akassa spoke again. "You were asked to come and kill us all."

"Yes, but they no longer call to me. The men, I mean." Asher asked her if she was feeling better then. "I am. I don't understand why I'm here. I have no desire to be a mate to anyone. I've been a slave to men all my life. Not sexually, but it would be just as bad. My sword is all I have ever had to offer to anyone. I have nothing else to give. My heart is now of stone, and black as the coal in yonder fire."

"We don't want you to be our slave. In fact, if you'd like, we could be yours." Akassa laughed when she looked at him, and Sally wanted to caution him. "We have a home that you're welcome to change in any matter that you wish. We're not slobs, but we'll do better, I promise you. You have only to ask for anything, and it will be yours."

"At what price?" Sally asked her what she meant. "Who do they wish me to kill? What army do I vanquish for them? No one wants me around but for my blade and armor. I'm a warrior, not a wife."

"Well that's just sad. And we don't want anything from you that you're not willingly ready to give." Sally could see the mistrust there, like a part of her armor. "You don't believe us. And that's fine too. I'm just glad that you're here. With us as family."

"My family is gone." Bryn stood up, and the men did as well. When she drew her blade the boys did too, but didn't point them at her, instead surrounding them all, ready for whatever had spooked the warrior. "There is someone coming."

Sally felt the magic tighten around her. She wasn't sure who it was from, but was glad for it. If there was going to be bloodshed, she didn't want it to be her family, but she thought them better suited to it than she might be. Holding onto Jacob, she was surprised to see Bryn standing next to her.

"They told me to stand here. I'm a warrior, don't they know that?" Sally nearly laughed, and might have had the girl not looked so murderous right then. "I'm not a milksop that needs to be protected. I protect them."

"Perhaps they are only looking out for your wellbeing, rather than you protecting them." Bryn said that was her duty. "Well, this is theirs. Their duty to protect their mate. Who's out there, Bryn?"

"A man and a woman. They're not human...wolf, I believe. And with the magic surrounding the land, they shouldn't have ill will in their heart if they were able to cross it, correct?" Sally said that was right. "Perhaps, but I do feel something about them. Something not right. I feel powerful magic, but it is wearing down. If there is ill will, it's being buried in the magic that surrounds them. We have to be careful of them."

"What is it?" They both turned to Asher when he spoke. "I have my children here...we all do. I'd like to know what we're up against."

"I can go to them." Asher looked at Simeon, and when he said she'd be the best for the job of protecting them, Sally was stunned by the smile that Bryn gave them all. "I'll protect them with my life. But the people out there, do not allow them in the house. Tinsel has gone to see what they're about."

Tinsel returned in seconds. He spoke to Bryn, who didn't seem any less tense for whatever he told her. Sally was going to have to brush up on her brownie language. She might have understood more if she did. But when Bryn told them what she knew, all thoughts of pulling out her books went out the door.

"They're wolves in sheep's clothing." Sally was fearful now for the young woman. "They've come here for me…they know that I'm here. They wish my services to help them kill humans. I shall have to go to them should they be allowed to see me."

"No." Asher looked around as he continued. "Akassa, take your mate to the caves. Kiaran, you take Simeon. The children will be fine with the faeries that are here now, so go before they see you."

"But I'm a warrior. My services are for anyone that needs them." Asher walked up to her and Bryn lifted her chin. Whatever happened next would be the turning point in this family, Sally knew it. "You wish to claim me, King?"

"Nay. You've been claimed by the King." She looked at her armor, then at him. "There. His mark is there. I saw it the first time I saw you. If I remember my laws of war correctly, you will fight for the next in line, without claiming, correct?"

"I've not been—" Sally saw it then too. As if saying the words, pointing it out, had made it clearer, brighter for them. "I didn't know. All these centuries, I've never seen it. I have been…. You must forgive me, my lord. I had no idea that I fought for others when I have been rightly claimed by another."

"We'll talk later. For now, I need for you to get away from here. We'll deal with this. Go." As she was bundled up in Akassa's arms, Asher turned to her. "Mom, I'd very much like you and Dad to go as well."

"Not on your life." She smiled at Jacob. "They're interrupting our dinner time, and they're not going to get off that easy. You go on out and see to them, Asher, my boy, and I'll be right there with you."

With a groan, Asher assembled the family. Sally wasn't afraid any longer, but smiling. This might be fun, she thought, and walked onto the newly decorated porch with her boys.

Chapter 3

Bryn paced the large cave. She had so much on her mind right now that she wasn't sure where to even begin in deciding what she was mad about. She'd been marked, and she'd never known about it. When Akassa laughed, she turned her temper on him.

"You do that well." She asked him what he was talking about. "Mumble and pace. I've only seen one other person do it that well, and I think you might be better at it than Asher. Only he doesn't mumble in several languages at once. Just one. What is it you're saying? Some of it I know, but the rest is older languages, I think."

"I shouldn't like being compared to the king, but I thank you for it. I know all languages. I can speak to any creature, shifter or not. In this, I can find out information that others might not be able to." He smiled at her, and it made her feel off. "You're very beautiful as a dragon. I haven't seen any in a great many years. There are many here?"

"Yes. Several hundred at last count. They're not all large

ones…in fact, most are about the same size as I am, but the larger ones are beautiful too." She wondered if he was making fun of her, but he only smiled again. "I can see your armor now. Before I could only see what a beautiful woman you were, but I can see it now."

"It's here because of the threat, and here I sit on a mountain top, waiting like some faint-hearted woman who knows not enough to get in out of the rain." Simeon laughed then. "You think to make fun of me?"

"No. I was thinking of you being faint of heart. I don't believe there is a person living that would be stupid enough to think that of you." Bryn didn't understand these men. They were nice. She sat, but far from them so they'd not touch her. Touching seemed to be a big part of their family when together. "You've been around longer than any of us. Longer than even my parents, I'm thinking."

"Longer than the king and queen from before." She stood up and looked at the walls that were sheltering them. Using her magic, she lit the way to the deeper part and asked them to follow her. They were perhaps thirty feet back when she showed them the walls there. "This is where I stayed when my parents were murdered. My sisters are there…my brother, Paul, as well."

The drawings on the wall had been done in her blood for the most part. There were bits of her family's as well. Their blood had mixed with hers when she'd found them, still abed. She remembered the day that she'd come here, the grief and pain that she'd poured onto these walls.

"My parents were still in their bed clothing. They'd been dead for only a few hours, their bodies still warm under the covers. My brother had been out of his bed, his body cut to ribbons, so he might have fought back, I think. He lost.... They removed his head and laid it beside him, as if he were looking up at me." Bryn touched the crude drawing of her little brother as she continued. "My sister, Beth and Rose, were abed too, but their bodies were mutilated as well. Beth had been killed with my brother's blade, a small one that he could handle. Rose had been.... They raped her. A child, and they raped her."

"Why?" She'd forgotten that they were with her, her grief so profound. "Why did they kill your family? I thought that they were under protection when you were away."

"They were. They were supposed to be, but the man that I worked for, a minor king who thought to expand his lands, decided that having me in his bed was going to be my next assignment. He knew then it was against the laws of my kind, but that mattered little to him. So, I left him there with his parts hanging out and injured." Simeon laughed again, and she smiled at him. "I wasn't too gentle with him in my telling him no. I think that is what spurred him to be so cruel to my family."

"No, I would imagine you weren't. So, it was him, that man, who killed them?" She nodded, looking at the drawings again. "I'm assuming that, as rights of war, you took care of him."

"I killed his household, as a matter of fact. Himself I have not yet found and killed." She turned from the memory and looked at them both. "I gave his family as much mercy as he'd given mine. They were all dead, the entire palace, within moments of me finding my family. Then I went back to my home only after his household were all dead, and buried my family in the gardens that my father so loved. There was no marker for them, for that I was sorry. But I think now, should I have done that, their graves might have been damaged. Then the house was burnt to the ground. After that...after that, I guess you could say that I gained more power. I shut my heart off to anyone. The pain I felt then, it's lessened very little. I cannot love you. Not as you would like."

"And how is it you think we want you to love us?" She asked Simeon what he meant. "Do you think that we want more from you than you're willing to give? That we'll make demands on you and your body that you wouldn't want? To me, that would be called raping you. No less than what happened to your sister. No, we want whatever you wish to give us. Share with us, no matter the subject, anything that you wish."

"That isn't how it works." He asked her how it worked. "I don't know, but you can't expect me to believe that you want nothing from me. I'm a woman, you're men. You will demand that I comply."

"If you think that we want you in our bed, then you're right, we do. Also, against the tree, the wall, even the ground if you were to consent. But we don't want you to give yourself to us because you think that is all we want. I want to talk to you. Be with you, around you. I'd like to wake up and know that we're going to be spending a great part of the day together. Those are the things I want. Do I expect them? Demand that you give them to us? No. I don't expect you to do anything unless you wish it." Simeon stood up, and she watched him walk toward her. Standing her ground, she didn't move, but itched to pull her sword and show him she wasn't going to be intimidated. "You're a very beautiful woman, sexy and strong, but you're also a woman who knows her own mind, her own heart. And that, more than anything, is what I want to get to know."

With a quick light kiss to her mouth, he left her there and moved out of the mouth of the cave. Looking at Akassa, she could see that he'd be no help at all. He was laughing quietly when he stood up.

"As much as I'd like to kiss you as well, I don't think you'll let it go a second time. But he's right. We are family now, no matter what brought us together. And I, for one, couldn't be happier with the outcome." She was still standing there when he left her as well.

For some reason, she didn't think they'd be far. After all, they did think to protect her. Bryn thought of all the things that she had on her person that would help her to care for them, and stomped to the front of the cave. Perhaps if she couldn't tell them to leave her alone, she could frighten them so that they would. But as soon as she came out of the opening, she stopped in her tracks. A dragon had come.

"Ada? I thought you dead." She hugged the great dragon, and felt her tears fall in knowing that she still lived. "Where is Dawood? I didn't think the two of you ever parted ways."

"He has died, mistress. He would so have loved to have seen you again." Bryn told her how sorry she was. "He was killed by the slayers. He saved my life when the iron was meant for me. But these people, they have made us a nice home here and have kept us safe. You are mated to these men? It is a grand thing to have such people love you."

Bryn glanced at the two men, wondering if they had perhaps asked her to say that. But Simeon thanked Ada and flushed with embarrassment. She knew then that the compliment was unexpected.

The two of them spoke for a while, Ada catching her up on things that she had missed and telling her of the others that were now there. A great many of the dragons that she thought had been killed had come to the magical land, and were being well cared for.

"Have you seen the new castle?" She told Ada that she had not. "You should see it. They've done a nice job of it. And the dragons, all of us, are pleased to be asked to help with the magic that the mountain needs. The former king and queen held so many things in its belly for the castle when it was rebuilt. It is like looking at the original one, only this one is bigger. And I think stronger for the lives that it now holds. The king Anthony, he did a wonderful job of making sure that we were all able to come here and live."

"I've brought the last book, but it seems to be without its own bit of mystery as well. It needs magic of some sort to make it work." Ada asked her if the book was plain. "Yes. You know it?"

"Aye, I have heard of it. We all have. It's the book of dragons. It can only be read by the one true king. I know very little about the actual book, but it is said to have all the names in it that were ever born, and then the names of those that died. Also, and I don't know this for sure, but it is said to have the diary of the king in it." Bryn asked Simeon and Akassa if they had heard that too, but neither of them had. "It would have been written well before they were born. Even the queen put her hand to it. But if the pages are blank, then I'm not sure how to read it. It would be a grand story, don't you think? I suppose you could ask them."

"Ask who?" When Ada didn't answer, she looked at the two men. "Who can I ask? The king and queen are dead, correct?"

"Oh yes, they're dead. But then, so were both our parents." She was confused by Simeon's words. "My father arrived here before we came to live here. I guess he was here all along, and talked with Elbert when he came. But then magic brought him to where we could all touch and see him. Then a few months ago, my mother came to see us. Lelani loved her very much, and was at her graveside when Mom appeared. Then.... Well, I can see this is very confusing for you. But trust me, the king and queen are here too. Just not solid. They won't be either. Something about their death."

"They died violently. Your parents, they died in their rest? Or perhaps of sickness?" Simeon told her that it was age and sickness. "But they're here, the king and queen are here where you can speak to them?"

"Yes, but not all the time. They need to rest when they use their magic to appear." Akassa laughed. "Why do I get the feeling that they're lucky that they're dead, that you have it in your head to murder them again? I'm thinking that they pissed you off a little?"

"They put me on this path without all the facts. I should like to speak to them about it. Also, why they picked me over everyone else, more suited to you two. As I stand here, I think of even more questions that I should like answers to." In fact, the longer she stood there, the angrier she got. Akassa stepped in front of her before she could go find them. "I need to speak to them."

"You do, and so do I, but there are people down there at my home that are risking everything to keep you safe. If you could just wait a bit more, at least until things are settled, then I'll take you to them myself." She asked him if he had questions as well. "Yes. Like why did they let you be harmed while working for them?"

The more she was around these people, the more confused she got. Why on earth would they care if she was hurt or not? And for that matter, why did they risk their lives to save her? She'd not asked them to do that. What would they wish in return for this supposed help she was getting from them? It bore thinking harder about.

~~~

Jacob sat quietly on the porch, but he felt his temper rising up with every word that came out of the man in front of him. He was flat out lying, and that wasn't sitting well with Jacob. There wasn't anything he hated more than a liar. Well, except somebody that hurt their wife and children. They were the worst as far as anything went. When the boys all came out and stood behind Asher, it was as if the man had come to realize that he might be biting off a bit more than he could chew up. Then the girls came out.

"I see you have company." Asher didn't bother looking, but said that they were his family. The man smiled a smile that didn't even come close to being friendly. It was like one of the dragons when they were upset. Showing a lot of teeth. "Family? My goodness, they're a large group. What are their names? Perhaps I'd like to meet them."

"No." Asher was pretty good at saying that single word and making it work. And when the man, he thought he said his name was Harrison, only stared at him, Asher smiled. "They're my family. That's about all you need to know."

"All right. Not very hospitable, are you? But I guess I can understand that. However, as I said, I was looking for Brynhilde. She was said to have come here. My son, you see, he hired her to do some work, and she's not been around to talk to him about it." Asher said nothing. "She's for hire, did you know that? It's in her blood to do as she is told. I'm sure she's told you that."

"I know all about her. And as for her being hired out, not anymore." Harrison puffed his chest out, like he had something powerful to say, and Asher cut him off. "Do you want to die? I mean, right here, right now? I can arrange that for you should you want it. The next words out of that lying mouth of yours had better be apologizing to me for insulting my sister-in-law."

Jacob wasn't sure if the man was madder than a hornet or just shocked. The look on his face now was something of both the feelings. But Asher, he just crossed his arms over his chest and waited. To ask a man when he wanted to die, Jacob thought that might need some considering.

"Sister-in-law? No, that's not right. She's not…. When did this come about?" Asher was good at staring a man down, and he did it to this one like it was his job. Jacob had to admit, he was right proud of his boy right then. "I demand that you bring her here right now so that I can bring her to my home."

Asher stood up, and when he did, the dragons on the porch shifted and his brothers took a step forward. Harrison took several steps back, and nearly fell over the man with him…his son, Jacob thought. He didn't have a clue who he'd been talking to, apparently.

"I'm Asher Benson, king of the dragons. What I do on my land is law. The dragons here are at my command, and you will live longer should you remember that." Old Harrison took several more steps back, bumping his fanny into his car. "My sister-in-law, Brynhilde, is now, and will forever be, under my protection. She has been claimed by the former king, and is thus now mine to do with as I see fit. If you come here again, I can assure you that she will gladly cut you apart without my permission, but I will gladly give it to her. Do I make myself clear? Or do I need to show you the force of my hand? Either way, it'll be fine by me."

"You're making a big mistake, dragon king. When I return, and you can bet that I will, she will be going with me when I leave you here in a puddle of your own blood. You and your family." Kiaran moved forward, the spew of hot flames burning the ground between Harrison's feet. "And leash your pets, dragon king, or they'll be the next thing on my list. You'll learn soon enough that to fuck with me is going to be the last thing you'll ever do."

After the man was gone, his car out of sight, Asher moved back up to the porch. He fell more than sat in the chair that was in front of him, and put his head on his hands. He was shaking hard by the time Jacob joined him, and he asked him if he was all right. Asher looked at him, and Jacob realized he'd been laughing, not crying.

"He shit himself." Jacob asked who had. "The son. He just dirtied his pants when Kiaran used his flame. I nearly fell over it was so funny. Can you imagine going home with that smell? And his father acting all brave and stuff when his kid had crapped his pants. I tell you, it was the funniest thing I've seen in a good long while. What do you think they'll do for an encore?"

"Well, I never." They all stood up as soon as Jacob's lady wife came out of the house. "To be having fun at someone's fearful expense. Asher, you should be.... You should be.... Oh dear heavens, did he actually do that?"

"Yes, ma'am, he did. Just as surely as I'm sitting here." Asher stood up and hugged his mom. "You would have beaten me within an inch of my life had I done anything like that, and I think I would have deserved it. But he is going to be trouble. Not that I'm worried about him, but he will be bothersome."

They were joined a few minutes later by the rest of the family, and the tale of what had happened was repeated. Even Bryn, who was a little standoffish, laughed a bit. Especially when the rest of them were having such a good time with it. Then they sat back down to finish their dinner, and Jacob could see that they were a little more relaxed around her then.

"They know that you're here. You have any idea how they would know that?" Bryn looked at Elam when he asked her. "I mean, they knew not only that you were here, but that we were dragons too. At least, I can only assume that they knew about us being dragons. He didn't seem surprised about that until his kid crapped his pants."

"I didn't tell them if that's what you're implying." He said that he wasn't, and smiled at her. "You're a strange bunch. Have you been told that before? You aren't at all like you're supposed to be."

"I believe that it's been mentioned before, and while I'm not sure you meant it as a compliment, I'm going to take it as one. But as for you telling anyone anything, I don't believe you would. I would stake my life on it. However, it still bears thinking about, that he knew you'd be here. Why, do you think? I mean, even if he knew of the dragons, that wouldn't have led him to think that you'd be here too. Especially since you were supposed to kill us for him."

"I cannot kill the dragons, nor the king. And as you are

all one person, dragon to man, I cannot kill any of you. Not even before this started." Casdon asked her why. "Because a dragon holds all magic; white and black, earth and air. Without them, or even without their magic, there would be nothing left of this world. The magic that they have, it sustains the earth and all her powers. It is told that all of the magics of the world were created by the dragons. A creature so strong and good that they even created Mother Earth so that they'd have someone to watch over them."

When she lifted her hand up, the world appeared. Jacob was in such awe of it, he nearly forgot to listen to her speaking. Bryn showed them how the cycle of the earth revolved. Not just the living, but the dead ones as well.

"Each time a dragon is killed or simply dies, there is a bit of their magic that goes back into the earth, even if their bodies are cut apart, the magic is still given. And when the dragon is killed by other means, such as man, then more of the magic goes into all the earth, not just the ground but all of the earth, to try and teach the inhabitants that killing such a creature is wrong." The view changed, and it became a world filled with lush trees, large plants, and animals. Among it were the houses of people, cave dwellers, and skyscrapers. Then it seemed to move, at dizzying speed, to where they were now, their little glen with the castle. "The magic holds them to this place. A place where they are not misunderstood nor killed for their properties, as well as magic. If they were all to die, even the smallest one, then all the earth would become a fighting ground for everything."

This time the scene changed from the lush to the devastated...burnt-out houses, dead bodies lying about, decaying. There were no trees, no plants that were viable. The ground looked as if it had been scorched dry, burnt to the point that nothing would grow there. He looked at Bryn as she continued.

"There are many humans that believe that they're responsible for the continuation of the earth. That cleaning up the air and water and making better cars are the thing that is helping the world. And they are, to a point. The dragons are more plentiful now. They are no longer hunted and killed. The dragon slayers, for the most part, have given up and moved on." Jacob pointed out that there were still some out there. "Yes, from the slayers from my time passing on the information, the need to kill them, to their own. It is, sadly, going to get worse before better. They will, if given the chance, kill everything in their path, only to be disappointed when even that does not satisfy their need for murder."

"What can we do?" She told Sally that they were doing all they could now. "But there is more. You know something that we don't."

"I do, and I'm afraid that you're not going to like the answer any more than you did those men coming here. I have to be contained. I am the last of my kind. The last warrior faerie to be able to draw a sword against them." Onimia asked her why she had to die. "Not die, I cannot, but I must be buried deep within a hold near water so that I cannot be brought forth. Because so long as I'm here, where I can be found, people are going to go after the dragons. I am drawing them to you. For this, I am profoundly sorry."

"There has to be a plan b." She shook her head at Akassa. "No, we'll think of something. And if not, then we'll be buried right along with you. Because as surely as I'm standing here, I'm not going to survive without you in my life now that

63

you're here. We do this together, or we'll be buried alive together. I'm all for suggestions on how to make this work."

"It's the magic." Everyone turned to look at Caroline when she came into the room and looked at Bryn. "My goodness, you've turned into such a beauty, my child. I heard that you were here. And I can't think of a better person than you to bring this all together. Now, we have to plan and play around a bit, and talk to Anthony and Eve. I'm sure that they might have a trick or two up their sleeves. And if not, we'll wing it, as I've heard said."

"Caroline." Bryn bowed before her, and didn't stand until Caroline touched her. "I have so missed you."

"And I you, child. Your parents would be so proud if they could see you now. I was sorry to hear about your family, but you have a good one now. Not to replace them, but to join you in this." Bryn said to her that they'd get hurt. "Yes, perhaps, but now that you're here, there is no chance for them to die. You brought that to them, and when you're mated to these fine men, you'll bring so much more. Gain more than you give. But that's not what's important at the moment, now is it?"

"My goodness, I think we might be able to pull this off." Everyone turned to look at Jacob when he shouted out his joy. "Yes, siree bob, I'm thinking that not only will we be all right, but we're gonna be better for it. Pass me the peas, love. I'm suddenly hungry as a bear."

Chapter 4

Harrison looked at his son. He'd been so proud of him when he'd gotten the warrior to work for them, and now this. There wasn't any way that he'd ever get the smell out of the car. He'd have to sell it, there was no hope for it now. Harrison Marsh would not tolerate embarrassment to his name, and his son had done that in a matter of minutes.

"Huston, you're going to pay for any cleaning I need done to this car. Christ. If I have to get rid of it after this, you're going to pay for that too. What the fuck is wrong with you?" Huston said he'd been terrified. "Well? What the fuck did you expect them to do? Let us come along and take them away? The next time I go there, I'm going to make sure you have a diaper on you. I'm betting that they got a good smell of you too while we were there. What a disappointment you are to me."

"They turned into fucking dragons, right there in front of us." He'd been startled by that as well, but he'd not shit himself over it. "They're bigger than you said, too. You said

65

they'd be small, like cats. And that fire? It came close enough that I could feel it like it was on me. Dad, you said that we'd be able to take them without any problems. Well, I see a huge fucking problem, don't you?"

"Well, I guess I was wrong, now wasn't I? But think of it this way, son, we're going to be rich when this hits the papers. And when that's all done with, the hoopla over finding them, then we'll cut them up for the parts. You said you know someone that deals in that shit, right?" Huston nodded, but still looked sullen. "Cheer up, buttercup. Your old dad is going to put our names out there."

"How you planning on doing that? If it's all the same to you, I don't want it to be in the obits part of the paper. You heard him, he's the king. According to the lore, he can keep the warrior from helping us. At least we know that part's right, don't we? Christ, this is going to be a shit party, I just know it." There was that, but Harrison chose to ignore it for now. Opening the window, he let some of the fresh air blow over him while Huston went on about laws and shit. "Also, you should know that what she told me about killing the dragons, she can't do that. Not even the king, nor his family. I didn't remember that until I came home and looked it up. She can no more kill the dragons than she can die. We're so screwed."

"Why not?" Huston told him. "You mean just because they're all one big happy family, we have to just walk away from this? I don't think so. She's been claimed by us, and she will damn well do as I tell her."

"It doesn't work like that, Dad. Once she's been marked, like I did to her, she has to work for us. And you should have told me that we'd have to touch her to get her claimed. I felt like an idiot when it happened. Then she pulled out that contract stuff to mess me up. Well, there ain't one that we have to sign, just in case she tries that again. But she would have had to do everything we told her. Even if it's something that is against the law, or if it's one of our own family we want dead." Harrison said that was what he wanted. "Yeah, but if she is claimed by the king, which that man said he was, then she has to do what he says over everyone else. It's sort of like he trumps our ace. And she will never be able to kill a dragon, nor cause them any harm for anyone. However, if they're trying to kill her, then all bets are off. And she's a true immortal."

"True immortal, huh?" He had no idea what that meant and didn't want to ask him, but he couldn't stand the fact that he wasn't informed. "What is the difference?"

"She can't be killed. No one can take her head off, or pierce her heart either. There is too much armor and magic surrounding her that would prevent anyone from doing that." Harrison asked how they contained her if she was bad. "They dig a hole and put her in it. Then they cover it with water. I'm not sure what all that means, but that will contain her for all time. Or until someone lets her out. She also has to hibernate when she's been hurt really badly. I think she sort of heals herself. And before you ask, it doesn't say how long she's down. I'm thinking the worse she's hurt, the longer she's down."

"Why do you know so much about this shit?" He told him he'd looked it up on the Internet, that there was a lot of it out there. "Oh, so most of this could just be bullshit, and the rest is a lie. I see. When you have some real facts, then we'll talk. Until then, you take a bath as soon as we get home and toss out those clothes. And when I want something told to me, things I already know, then I'll find you. Christ, you stink like you've shit yourself. Oh wait, you did."

Harrison was going to do his own investigating. After finding all that crap at an auction about six months ago, when the brotherhood had gone under, he'd thought it would be a lark to go and see about these dragons. But the couple of people that had been there, when it supposedly went down, had said that there had been real dragons and that they'd had fire for breath, as well as enough strength to tear a man apart. He'd only believed about half of that shit, but it had made him want to look harder. And he had turned up some pretty convincing arguments for getting hold of a dragon. The riches were what he was hoping for.

When they got home, he didn't even bother pulling into the garage. Not that anyone would complain about his piece of shit in the driveway again. He'd nipped that in the bud a few years back. The society that ran their development had given up on him getting shit down on time and keeping his yard according to their rules. He hated them, for the most part, and their rules. The one that caught up in his craw was the trashcan one.

His service had run out a few months back, so, in order to not have trash piling up so that the damned raccoons couldn't get into it, he'd been having the boy take the trash out and put it in some of the cans around the neighborhood the night before pick-up day. That had worked out really well for them until someone told on him. Harrison realized that he should have been better at hiding his address by not throwing his mail into the lot. But come on, people, it was trash, for Christ's sake. But he'd been told to stop, and had even gotten a fine. Like he was going to pay that.

To his way of thinking, his house was just that, his. He paid his taxes on the place. Made the payments when he could, anyway, and he mowed when the grass was too high for him to find his chair. Besides, his house had been there first, not theirs, and they should be following his rules, not making them up as they went along.

The house was a mess too. Not just the yard, where he did somewhat take pleasure in making that area of his living space a little trashier than he would normally have. But the inside, the place where him and the boy slept and ate, was nasty. Even he was aware of that. Since Huston's mother had run out on him a few years back, saying that he was a slob and a pain in her ass, he'd just not had the energy nor the inclination to do much of anything that meant housework to him. He didn't like to do any job, but housework was a bitch, and he couldn't make Huston do it either.

Not that he was thinking it was all a woman's job. No, his mom had raised him to know that work was work, and everyone messed up and so everybody did the cleaning. But he hated it with a passion. Dishes, laundry, and anything that related to him cleaning up, he just didn't want to do. Even going so far as getting paper plates when there was money for them, and cups too. But that only generated more trash, which was a problem too. It was like one of them catch twenty-one things. Or whatever the number was. But he was in a pickle with it.

It was nearing midnight when he got on the computer. It wasn't his. He'd snatched it a while back when someone had left it out on their porch. He knew that they insured those kinds of things, so taking it when he needed it so badly hadn't bothered him overly much. But then, rarely did things bother him overly much anymore about his neighbors and their crap. As he looked up about dragons, the first thing he saw was the number of books about them. Then he realized it was romance shit.

"Christ almighty. Don't people have enough to do without going out and reading this crap?" But he found himself intrigued by some of the covers, and before he knew it, he'd picked out several that he was going to see if he could get sometime. Not having a credit card was the only thing that prevented him from getting them right then. One by Julia Mills had him thinking he might be working harder on getting it. It looked good.

He had been able to read a bit of her work...it was something that he might have seen his wife reading. Sexy covers and the men looking like they could just stare you into whatever they wanted of you. Harrison had them in his wish list thing, and even unmarked some of the other shit he had in there so he could get them first.

The sun was coming up when he realized that he didn't have a clue what he was doing. Yeah, there was a lot of information out there about dragons and shit, but nothing he could use. He decided to pull out the books he'd gotten at the auction and read up on them. At noon, he found what he'd been searching for.

Huston had been right, about all the shit he'd been spouting. Not only could she not be killed, but it sounded like nobody believed that her kind were around anymore. That even if you could find one, a warrior faerie, convincing them to do what you wanted might be harder than it seemed. There were rules about how to go about that, too.

He had to touch her armor. It didn't say where it might

be, but touching it would bind her to you. And if she was touched by a king, the only mark there'd be would be a little thumbprint, smaller than his pinky finger. He wasn't sure how one was supposed to see something so tiny, but he guessed that like the rules, it was meant to be confusing. Harrison read on to come to understand why it was so small.

"To ensure that the other kingdom will not know who had sent her." Seemed kind of silly to him, but then this whole thing was a might off. "Once she has done the deed that has been asked of her, she is to be paid the equivalent of her weight in gold. If she is not paid, then the holder will forfeit something or someone of great value to the holder of the warrior."

So, she might have to take his kid, if he weighed as much as she wanted. But then, it only said that she would take something, not that it had to weigh as much as her. Harrison wondered if that meant she was wearing her armor, if she had any. He thought that would add a considerable amount to her if so. But he was thinking that she'd end up with his kid. There wasn't any gold to be had in this family, much less weighing out as much as she might.

He glanced over at his son, who was currently eating a bowl of what looked to him like puke in a bowl. Where he'd gotten the milk or the cereal was beyond him. Just last night he'd asked after some milk for his coffee, and had been told there wasn't any. Now his own kid was lying to him. Then he found what he'd been looking for. A breakdown of a dragon.

The prices on a whole dragon were a lot more than he'd thought...like thousands more than he would have guessed. Of course, he'd not believed there was one out there, so he'd not really looked for any prices, but the breakdown on them,

71

the volume of things that could be taken off a dragon, was inconceivable. Even if the scales alone were correct in number and price, he'd be a rich man forever.

Harrison hadn't had a great deal of schooling. He'd graduated, but it wasn't because he'd been smart enough to do so. It was more like he'd bullied his way through. And when he'd turned twenty, he'd been given his diploma and sent home. The stupid thing still hung in his bedroom on the wall.

Huston had dropped out the moment he'd turned sixteen and never looked back. Not that it bothered Harrison all that much. Not having to buy school shit for him and new clothing had been a relief. But he'd kept up with reading, so Harrison was sure Huston was smarter than he was now. Not that he'd tell him that. And he could do math in his head faster than Harrison could bring it up on a calculator.

Anyway, Harrison could understand that the things he was seeing here, that he was going to have to work hard for it. Not just that, but he might get himself hurt too. Not that he was afraid of pain or nothing, but he didn't want to linger with it. Those dragons were big, and while he was too, they were strong and he was fat.

When his son left for his job, whatever the hell he did all day, he got himself out a piece of paper and a pencil and began figuring out what he would need and needed to do. Surely the first thing had to be to get more people. Even if he could do the rest of this on his own, he couldn't very well wrestle down a dragon. But they had to be good people, not like his neighbors.

"Got to be able to trust that they don't think I'm nuts." Harrison chuckled. "I am, I guess, if I try this, but the money will convince everyone that I'm not."

By the time he was done with his list, he'd figured out a few things too. He had to get himself a bigger car, not to mention one that ran every time you turned the key. There also needed to be a first aid kit nearby.

Telling people what he had once he had the dragon would get him arrested. No one, it seemed, believed that there actually were dragons, except this group called Death to all Dragons. It took him an extra ten minutes to figure out that that had been the name of the group that had disbanded a few months back. But there was a bigger organization, one that seemed to have plenty of money, if their ad on the computer was anything to go by. He decided that they were his best bet in getting information on the dragons and how to bring one down. And he was going to do it too. Even if he had to give someone his kid to make it happen.

Writing down the email address that they had there, he got him another piece of paper and wrote out what he wanted the email to say. He wasn't so much worried about his spelling on the computer. The thing all but did the writing for him when he had to get it right. Harrison didn't want to come off sounding like a fool. For all he knew this group could be about killing off dragon flies, the nasty things that flew in his face when he was just out walking around.

It took him twenty minutes to get his letter straight, then another ten to get it all typed into the computer. He was exhausted by the time he was finished, and staggered to the bed. He knew that he wasn't going to hear from anyone, knowing that they were just as dumb as the rest of the world, and had thought their name was cool. Harrison had already figured out that they more than likely sold shoes or hats or something equally dumb. It was hard to tell about things like that when there was nothing to see but a computer ad.

~~~

Huston had his own plan where the warrior was concerned. He was going to use her just as his dad wanted, but he was going to be getting himself a little on the side too. Or a lot. Then when he was finished with her, which he doubted would be anytime too soon, he was going to sell her off to his buddies. To hell with fucking with those dragons right away. He didn't need money badly enough to be killed over it.

The woman had been sexy as fuck standing there with her sword out. He'd felt his cock stretch out in his pants like she'd touched him when he'd thought of her last night. The thought of her sucking him off was almost more than he could think about, and when he had, he'd come so hard in his hand that he thought he'd broken something important. But as soon as he thought of her again, his cock had gotten hard once more, like it'd not just jizzed all over him.

The notes that he'd been stashing away when he found them were very helpful. Huston had been reading all kinds of things to do to get the king to release her to him. And he was pretty sure that he had a good plan, at least one that would benefit him. All he had to do was convince that big guy, without the dragons around, that he wanted her only for sex and not for the dragons.

It was a big lie, of course. He would eventually get around to the dragons. Just not yet. He wasn't stupid enough to not want that sort of money. And there was going to be a lot of it too. Huston wanted to make her like him, trust him first, so that if they did try to burn him up again, she'd be there on his side to protect him. Huston wasn't as naïve as his father.

"Like he's going to be able to kidnap this woman, make her do what he wants, and ignore the fact that she has these dragons on her side. Not just her side, mind you, but she might even be able to call on a bunch of them." Huston smacked at the snowman that was sitting in the front yard of his neighbor's house. "Stupid holidays."

He was bitter with his dad for not even wanting to put up a tree this year. Not that there'd be any gifts under it, nothing that his dad would go out and get for him. But it would have been nice to have a tree, damn it. Mom used to put one up even if she was sure there wasn't going to be any pretty papered wrappings under it. His mom was the best.

"Yeah, so good that she left you behind, didn't she?" That wasn't really right. He'd been in jail when she'd left them. There wouldn't have been any way for her to have taken him with her, and now that he was out, he didn't have a clue where to find her. She was hiding from Dad, he knew that. His dad had a mean fist, but not against him anymore.

Huston had learned to defend himself while in jail. Not just from the bullies, but the would-be lovers too. He didn't roll that way, yet it mattered little to them. But he'd gotten out with his cherry, as it was called, and he was careful now to make sure that he didn't get caught and end up back there. Not getting caught was the way to go. And if he was unlucky enough to get his ass back in the jail, this time he wasn't going to call his dad, nor was he going in empty handed. He knew how to make himself a knife now.

Dad had come down to the jail to see him. But he'd laughed at him and made fun of the fact that he'd been caught. Not even telling the police that it had been his dad's fault had done him any good either. He'd been the one that had been caught with the goods, not his dad. The fucker was going to pay for that too, someday soon.

Huston had made no friends while he'd been serving time for robbery, and he had even fewer now that he was out again. His dad was to blame for most of that, too. He was forever picking fights with people that he had no intention of fighting with. Huston figured that it made him feel like a big man when they backed away from him. Whatever. Huston could and would fight if it was necessary, but to his way of thinking, there wasn't much out there that was worth getting all banged up for.

As he sat up his station to wash up dishes, he thought of all the things he could be doing right now. Nothing, he thought with a grin. He'd be either sitting on the couch watching stolen cable with his dad, or sitting in his room looking at the four walls. Either one didn't pay him.

"I need the salad plates run through first, then some of the silverware. We got backed up this morning when the dishwasher repair guy had to be called in." Huston said he'd get right on them, and started loading the smaller plates onto the rack as his boss stood there. "What are your plans after you get off work tonight?"

"Go home, I guess. You got something else for me to do?" Roger said that he did, he'd talk to him later. "All right then."

As much as he hated doing such a sloppy job, he did enjoy the way the dishes came out on the other end all shiny and clean. They were chipped and in bad shape for the most part, but he treated them like they were fine china. When his break came, he sat at the little table in the back and played around with the newspaper. He could read it, and he did so, front to back without missing a single thing. It helped him pass the time as well as keep him updated on his surroundings.

A burger and fries were set in front of him just as he was giving up on trying to figure out what the mayor had done now.

"I was told you were getting this." He nodded but didn't touch it yet. He wasn't so stupid as to think he was getting something for nothing. "Go on, eat it. Roger said to give it to you. It was ordered and then not wanted."

"Has it been out to the table?" Sharon said it hadn't. "You expect me to believe that someone ordered this, and Roger said to give it over to me? What's the catch?"

"Don't know that there is one. He asked me if I wanted it. I don't eat red meat. He asked James too, and he said no way. So, if you think he singled you out, he didn't. We all got asked before you did." He picked the burger up and knew that something was up. "I got you a cola too if you want it."

"Sure." The burger was still hot, and the French fries were steaming enough to burn his tongue, but he ate it all before she came back with his drink. It was the first meal, hot or cold, that he'd had, other than cereal, in a long time. That was another thing that had changed when his mom had left them…nobody could cook like she did.

Roger came in just about the time he was ready to go back to work. When he sat, Huston stood up. He was waiting on him to speak, but not that long. Huston wasn't going to lose his job over a burger, no matter how good it tasted.

"Your dad tried to get in touch with an organization that I belong to." He asked him what that had to do with him. "A great deal, as a matter of fact. You know of the dragons. I'm with the group Dragon Slayers."

Huston sat down. He wasn't sure what to think about

this, but he figured that if his dad had inquired about them, then he might as well listen. Roger handed him a pamphlet.

"No thanks, I'm not interested in anything you might have there." He pushed it back at him. Roger said he'd read it to him. "Don't bother. I could read it if I wanted, but I don't care. I don't know what this is all about, but I got me some plans of my own concerning the woman. She's gonna be mine."

"You mean the faerie warrior? She will eat you up and spit you out again. She's too much even for me, and I've been training to deal with people like her. Did you know that she's an immortal? That you can't kill her?" He said that he did know that. "All right. Do you know what you have to do to contain her? It's not as easy as it might look."

"What do you want with her? I'm assuming by the name of your club, you plan on killing off the dragons. She can't do that. She told me." Roger told him that she had killed one. "She was under attack. I'm guessing that was you guys. How did you get a dragon to help you? I mean, they know what you're doing, right?"

"You ask a lot of questions for someone that doesn't know a great deal." He wasn't sure where Roger had gotten that information, but Huston let it go. "She killed the dragon that was a part of my plan. And as for how we got him to cooperate, that's none of your concern either."

Huston stood up. He wasn't sure he was going to have a job after this, so he decided that he'd just tell the guy like he saw it. There was just too many people going after his woman, and he didn't care for it.

"She's out at the property that the Bensons live on. I've never been there myself, but I heard that it's just about the nicest land around. And when they come into town for stuff, they're all right to people. I just want the woman. They can have the dragons. They're too nasty for me anyway." He backed away, watching his boss. Huston had been out there, but he wasn't going to tell him that. Nobody needed to know that he'd shit himself over them monsters. "Do I still have a job here? Or was the burger dinner my last?"

"You have a job, but I want you to think about this, Huston. As a single person, you don't stand a chance in hell of getting that woman to come to you. But as a group, an organized one that has the weapons to deal with her, we can get her to do whatever you want. Even if that means fucking you." He felt his face heat up but didn't comment. "Just think about it. And yes, you have a job here. For as long as you want."

After Roger left him, Huston went to his station. He stood there for several minutes, thinking about what he'd been told. She had messed with them a little, and she had told them that she'd not be able to kill the dragons. But as far as fucking him went, he wasn't sure about that either, to be honest. She was a really pretty woman, but she was also hard, and he'd bet she liked sex the same way. Yeah, he might be better off with a group to get her, but he'd wait before telling Roger. No since in letting him think he just caved. Doing the dishes that were piled up, he started to whistle. Things were looking up for him, he thought. Finally.

Huston had been working at the little diner for about three years now. The job wasn't that hard; it was long hours of standing on his feet, but it gave him money to buy things he wanted. Shoes and a coat. Sometimes he'd buy himself one of the microwave dinners. But eating that at home, or even storing them there, had been hard. His dad usually found them, or wanted one too when he was eating them.

At midnight, when he was ready to clock out, he'd come up with a plan for how to get some things for himself. If this group was organized, then they'd have some money. Money that he could sure use about now. Getting himself a place of his own, with his own things, wasn't the first thing on his list when he'd started out, but it had moved up more and more when he thought of the shit going on at his house. This was something that he thought he deserved too.

Also, he wanted to be fed every day that he came to work. Not just burgers, but a steak and a baked potato once in a while. His list had been really long when he'd started naming things to himself that he wanted, but it was narrowed down now. There was no point in getting greedy, not like his dad would have been. And that was something on his list too. He didn't want his dad to be any part of this deal. Not one thing. He was pretty sure that he'd muck it all up for him anyway.

Huston was surprised to find Roger out in the parking lot. After telling him to get into his car, Roger started the engine but didn't move. He looked at Huston and asked him what he wanted to do.

"I'll help you all out, but I have some things that I want too. Like some cash. I'm tired of going hungry and cold." The engine sounded smooth, not at all like the piece of shit he had before. Roger's smile made Huston think he wasn't getting shit. "And I don't want my dad in this. He's greedy and an ass. It's me or him."

"I can work with that, and I have a grand here for you too. Can't have our best man starved and cold, now can we?" He wasn't sure if he was being pranked or not, but smiled when a thick envelope was handed to him. "You'll get that once a week until we get her. Then the money will be ten times that much. Welcome to the Dragon Slayers, Huston."

Chapter 5

Simeon watched the two of them as they worked in the yard. He'd gotten up this morning and found the house empty but for him and Akassa. After searching the house, he'd gone out to the porch to find Bryn working with Mark and his sword. The two of them were doing well, he thought. Akassa joined him, giving him a plate of food.

"Do you suppose she's eaten?" Akassa said that there was a clean plate in the drainer, as well as a fork and a glass. "Good. To be honest with you, I was afraid that she didn't eat. You know, being what she is, I just didn't know."

"She bathes too. Her towel was hung up over the hooks, and her dirty things were in the hamper. I'm not sure if she brushed her teeth, but she is clean." Simeon glared at his counterpart, but ate instead of talking. "By the way, what she's teaching Mark, she got permission from his parents before starting. I thought that was nice of her."

"It's sort of an art, isn't it? I mean, the way she's having him move with the sword. How he falls, even, isn't as bad as I think I'd do. I've been watching them for a little while now, and all I can think about is music. That if what they were doing had music playing in the background, I'd go see it as a play." They watched Mark fall again...well, be tripped, he supposed. "He doesn't get angry with her either when she does that. I wonder if she told him that if he did, she'd stop. Or maybe she'd cut him to ribbons. Perhaps that's what she'd say to us. A kid might be a little different."

She looked in their direction, and he had a feeling that she knew they'd been watching her all along. Setting down his plate, he and Akassa walked the length of the yard to see what they could learn. But as soon as they were close enough, he heard her tell Mark that he needed to bond with his sword.

"What does that mean?" She told him that he and his sword weren't one person. That he needed to make sure that it wasn't just something to keep him safe, but that it knew what to do almost before he did. "Okay, I'm still not sure what that means."

She looked at him, and he could see that she was trying hard to explain without making him feel bad. Simeon nodded at her and told her that if she told him, perhaps he could help her.

"He has to feed it. You and Akassa, you're one person when need be, correct?" He nodded. "Okay, this sword was a gift to him, from the former king. The sword became...I guess you could call it neutral. It has no owner, nor does it feel like it's part of a person. For all it knows it could be sitting on a shelf someplace. To bond with it, it'll know your thoughts, your hurts, and your fear. And fear is a good thing. I'm afraid every time I draw my own. But with it, drawn or not, I feel better because we're a single unit when we go to battle."

"So, you're saying that it has life?" She said sort of, but it was more than that. "Can you explain it? I'm sorry, but I'm trying my best to understand this. This is all new to me too."

"A person's sword is like an extension of them. Like the dragon is for you. When you need him, Akassa is there for you. The sword isn't any different." She asked for his sword, and Mark handed it to her with a smile. It occurred to him that Mark was smitten with Bryn, but he was trying to understand this right now. He'd deal with the young man later, if it came to that. "See the markings on this blade? They were made by a faerie. Also, it looks as if maybe the queen of the faeries has had her hand on it too. And a troll. That's what the blade is made of, troll saliva."

"Eww. Are you kidding me?" She shook her head at Mark. "You mean that some troll someplace spit on this thing?"

"No, it's actually his spit. When he helped make this sword, he spit a long spittle of himself on an iron table and forged it from that." Mark made a gagging sound that made them all laugh. "This is the finest sword you could ever hope to use. Not only is it made with troll spit, but there's—"

"If you tell me that someone has peed on it, I'm never touching it again. That's the most disgusting thing I've ever heard of." Bryn laughed, and Simeon nearly fell back. It was the most beautiful sound he'd ever heard. "What else is on it? Something's poop? Or maybe vomit? I thought it was just a sword that would be nice to have. I love that the king gave it to me, but to have someone's spit on it is one thing. A man's poop is really gross."

"Nothing like that. It has blood in it." Instead of grossing the young boy out, it seemed to brighten him up a little. "The blood of the faerie queen is what made the markings. The brownie that gave the handle has put his initials here on the pummel. And since it's in brownie language, not everyone would know that he was the greatest sword maker ever born. Also, you might believe this or not, most of the swords made today are made by a brownie. And the lines here, the ones that look like writing, are not only the names of the people that made it, but those who have used it. The king used this, as well as his wife. Each time a person bonds with it, their name, in the language of the faeries, is put here too. A part of the sword that will never go away, be broken, nor reformed with someone else's marks."

"Okay, that's cool. And now, when I feed it, I'll have my name on there too." Bryn nodded. "How do I do that? Pee or spit?"

He giggled, and while he wasn't sure what he was going to have to do to bond with the sword, Simeon knew that it was going to be something else. Pee or spit wasn't anything that the sword would understand. He watched Bryn when she knelt to Mark's level.

"Blood." No one moved. And while he could understand the concept, he was a little freaked out by the thought of Mark bleeding on the sword. "All you need to do is nick your thumb or finger and rub it over the scroll work. Once you do that, the sword will belong to you and no one else. And it will conform to you. It will be a part of all that you are. Even as you grow, so will the sword. If you are hurt and cannot carry it for some reason, it will know and adjust to fit your needs."

"And what happens when his mom finds out? I don't think she'll have a problem with it, but we should —" Simeon was shaking his head at Mark doing this, but it was too late.

Mark ran his thumb down the blade, then rubbed the

blood over the scroll work, just like he'd done it a million times. Before Simeon could find out if he was all right, the sword started to hum, then it turned a bright blue. All the time it was going through the change, Mark held onto it with both hands and didn't stop smiling.

When he fell to the ground, Simeon started to reach for him when Bryn told him to wait. He didn't appear to be hurt in any way, so he did wait. She would know better than anyone, he supposed, if something had happened to the boy. After several minutes Mark stood up, but he looked beaten… exhausted, he supposed. When he staggered over to the porch where they'd been sitting, he sat down, holding the sword in his lap like a lifeline. He looked up at him when he said his name.

"I'm okay. I'm feeling really sleepy, but I'm all right. I don't hurt at all, I'm just wobbly." Simeon sat next to him while Bryn stood in front of him. "That was fantastic. I guess that we're okay now, the sword and me?"

"Yes. Would you like to try it out?" Simeon wasn't sure that was such a good idea, but Mark stood up and held out the sword. "Just think of how I've been teaching you. How to hold the sword. Where it has to be pointed when you're setting your feet. It's a weapon, as I told you, so you must always be concerned where you have the blade pointed. If you do not, then you could hurt someone, or yourself. Carefully think about each movement of yourself and the blade."

Simeon could see that he was better at it. Not only did Mark hold the sword steadier, but his movements were smoother, his muscles didn't seem to strain so hard. As Mark practiced with Bryn, Simeon reached out to his brother to let him know what was going on.

She already let us know what she's been doing and what Mark has done. And she had Mark make sure it was okay with us as well. As for the sword, I knew that eventually he'd have to do that, and I'm glad that you guys were there when it happened. He's doing well, then? Simeon told him he was doing very well. *I knew he would. And to have someone like Bryn training him on how to do it, that's even better.*

He told him that he'd record some of it for him and pulled out his phone. Simeon had been in awe of the things she was doing before, but after Mark had fixed his sword, they were in perfect harmony with each other. The music that he'd thought of before this was now almost an opera, something that he would pay good money to see.

"Do you think that she'll be like that in bed?" Simeon looked at Akassa. "The reason I ask is, she's so focused on what she's doing. And all I can think about is how she'd touch me or you. I'm not being a pervert, but I do want to know if she'll touch me that way too…that's all. Christ, she's beautiful."

"You're not a pervert, and we're not going to ask her either." Akassa said that he wasn't going to. "But you're right. If she puts as much effort into making love as she is teaching him those movements, then we're going to die. Happily, but dead all the same."

They were both still laughing when Mark made his way home. There was plenty for them to be doing—the castle still had a few things they could finish up—but for right now, they were enjoying sitting on the deck with her. She sat on the chair and the two of them shared the swing. Simeon thought he could very easily get used to this. Just being family without all the worry of being something more.

"He's very good...focused and willing to learn. Men that I had to work with have never taken to the sword as readily as he did. And he's very smart as well. Did you know that he's thinking of becoming an attorney? He seems to think that there will be a need for dragon representation. I didn't tell him that they already had their representation, but he's happy." He asked her if it was Asher. "No, it's all of you, including the mates to you. The king, it's his duty to watch over them. Make sure that they're cared for and happy. Asher does a good job of that. I've never seen so many of them happy with the way things are going. But you all, with your dragons and magic, you represent them in the best possible way by keeping them safe, and rules enforced. King Anthony did a good job, but he lacked help and had to do everything for himself. This is much better."

"I sometimes forget that you were here during that time. When there were lots of dragons. What was it like? I mean, we have it now, but there are so many more people around too." She nodded and looked out beyond the trees. Simeon wasn't sure she was going to answer him.

"When I was little, about eight or so, the skies were filled with them. Not just the larger ones—it might surprise you to know that there weren't that many of them—but the little ones too. The slayers have been around since about the time the dragon was first created. And when they started to hunt them, it was harder and harder for them to take to the skies. The smaller ones, they could and often did pass for birds, or even smaller flying animals. But the larger ones, with no planes or such to mistake them for, they began to take more and more to the grounds. Ada and her brother, they were only about as big as you are when you're your dragon when

89

I was little." She leaned back in her chair, her head resting on the back as she continued. "When the king and queen took to the skies, if only to survey the grounds, it was such a glorious sight. Their colors were so brilliant, and it almost hurt one to see them there. A lot of the other dragons would do that as well, take to the skies just to say that they'd flown with the king and queen. Of course, that wasn't quite right, but no one cared then. It was a pleasure to be with them."

"I guess you had a strange childhood, what with being a warrior." She nodded and smiled at him. "You're very beautiful when you do that. It's like the sky has opened up and shone right down on you. There are times when I'm amazed at how lucky we are to have you in our lives."

"Would you kiss me?" Simeon didn't move, nor did Akassa. "You don't have to. I mean, it's not that big of a deal, but I've never been kissed. Not once. My parents, they were afraid of me. I would never harm them, but when I was little they were afraid of making me upset or something. When I got older and started to get called upon, it was sort of too late for us. It was like the habit was never there for us to hug or show affection, so it didn't begin then. They weren't mean to me or anything. I knew that they loved me, but I wasn't loved on like the others."

"I'm sorry." She shrugged and Simeon felt bad for the child she'd been. "You should have seen our household. There was never a minute that went by that we weren't hugged or loved on. I can't imagine not being hugged at least once a day. My mom and dad, they still hug us, tell us that they love us. It's the most amazing feeling."

"My father wasn't affectionate anyway, but my mom was. She would hug a person she didn't know if she felt they might benefit from it. I was jealous for a long time about that. How she could hug others and not me. But then I realized how much different I was from them. Not just because of the armor and such, but I had all these magical spells hidden over my body that were just as lethal as the sword and my knife." She smiled sadly. "I didn't blame her for it. But Paul, my brother, he would hug me when he could. There were times when I'd have to push him away, and I'd hate it. But the magic that made me strong would be too much even for me after a horrendous battle. I miss them, but mostly him."

"What do you mean about them being over your body and hidden?" She stood up and he watched her run her hand over her arm. When she pulled her hand away, she not only had a knife in her palm but also a star, something that she'd throw at her enemy. "Those are a part of your skin?"

"Yes. I have them hidden now, but if I wanted, or you did, I could show you. They were part of what I got from the king that night. Or the queen. I'm not sure. Every place on my body is a weapon that I can use. And most of them are forever ready to use. Like the guns, which didn't come around until they were invented. As soon as something new comes along or I hear about it, I have it upon my body. Sometimes it replaces the older version, sometimes it just upgrades it. Then there were the spells too." She leaned over and pulled a small vial from her thigh and handed it to him. "That is for sleeping. A small drop can put a full-grown troll to sleep for hours."

While they watched, she let her body go...*became* was all he could think of. She became all that she was, a warrior. The weapons that looked like tats weren't just appearing on her, but it looked as if they were being created over her. The lines were drawn, then filled in, shaded, and the detail was startling. Color was added to things that might need them. The detail on the gun was striking. It looked so real, so lethal that he was afraid for a moment. The blade at her hip was long and sharp, and when she pulled it free, he could see how useful it would be in a fight. It was barbed and thin. Bryn explained that most of the weapon was covered in magic, as well as poisons should it become necessary. She then showed them her armor.

"It got stronger as I got older, the more wars that I fought for my owners. There were times when I was sure it weighed more than I did. But it never failed me, nor did it get dented or stained. I think now that I know he touched me, the king might have done that. I've since changed my mind about screaming at him like a harpy when I see him." Bryn smiled at them. "I still might have to give him a little talking to about bringing me here under falsehood. And I hope that he will understand that some of the things I did, I did so because I didn't know that he'd claimed me that night. I fought for others when I was claimed by him, and that is an unforgiveable law."

"I'm sure that he'll understand," Akassa told her. "And Asher has forgiven you for that anyway. And not harping on Lord Anthony might be a good thing. But then, Dad might enjoy a good fight. From what I've heard about him, he loved to argue." Bryn nodded but looked sad. "Did I say something wrong?"

"No. I guess I'll start on the castle now. I mean, there isn't much I can do until the rest of the work is done, but I can help with the trees and such." They stood up when she backed from them. "You guys have a good night."

"What about the kiss?" Simeon was sure when he saw her face that she'd thought they didn't want to do it. "I'd love nothing more than to feel your mouth beneath mine. Touch you with my fingers."

"And I can't think of anything I'd rather do than to hold you in my arms. It's all I've thought about." Akassa touched his fingers to her cheek as he continued. "Your skin is so lovely. And when you change into your other self, I want to touch you then as well. I love you, Bryn."

Her moan was nearly their undoing. When she closed her eyes, all he could think about was seeing her lying between them, her body lax after them making love to her all night. Simeon wanted to feel her beneath him. Touch her in ways that no one else but him and Akassa would.

"I'm not like the others." Simeon asked her who she wasn't like. "The other women in this family. I'm a warrior; I have more blood on my hands than all of you do in your bodies. I'm not soft or sweet. I don't know how to decorate something. Flowers or chocolates aren't going to sway me. I'm not at all like other women you might know."

"That's an odd thing to say, but right now all I want is to touch you. We don't want you to be like the other women. We need you to be you. What you are. That is the person we both fell in love with. Neither of us want you to be anything or anyone but who you are. Never fake it with us."

Akassa moved behind her when Simeon stood to her front. Her breathing was quick, like she was nervous or out of breath. His own heartrate was speeding up, and he didn't want to mess this first time up with her. Even if all they got to do was kiss her, touch her, it was going to be their first, and he didn't want her to be overwhelmed. Like he was at the moment.

"Kissing is so intimate." He told her that it was. "I think

you two are going to be too much for me. I don't know why, but I'm afraid of you both. Not of you, I guess, but about you. What you're going to do and expect of me in this."

"We'd never hurt you. And we only want what you want to give us." She said that she knew that. "And we'd never do anything, ever, that you didn't want or enjoy."

"Kiss me." Simeon did. He brushed his mouth over hers gently. The hunger that he'd been holding back for days shot forward, and he had to let out a long breath or do just what he didn't want, rush her. But when she pulled his face to hers and devoured him, he heard Akassa laugh and knew he was a goner. Pulling back to look at her, he could see it...her need matched his own. "I feel...I feel overwhelmed, and need you at the same time."

"Good. That's about how we feel all the time around you." He kissed her again, showing her his hunger for her. His need too. When she moaned against his mouth, he lifted his head to look at her again. Akassa wasn't going to wait either, it appeared. He had her blouse unbuttoned and her sleeve pulled down so that he could nibble on her neck.

Her breasts were there, just peaking beneath the blouse that she had on. He opened it to see what treasures she had there and his knees nearly buckled. She was beyond beautiful. And she was theirs.

They were exposed out here, on the porch like they were, so he pulled back. Not to stop what they were doing, but to take it some place more private. Her blouse was off, her breasts were bared now, and all he wanted to do was taste her. So he did. Simeon leaned in and took the morsel into his mouth so that he could taste her.

"Please." He nodded to her and lifted her into his arms.

Akassa moved to the door, but before he opened it, he leaned over her and took her breast into his mouth and suckled loudly. "You're killing me. One of you has to do something, anything, to relieve this...pressure. I'm going to implode if you don't."

Taking her into the house wasn't as easy as it might have been had any of them not been trying to undress the other. Before they were to the couch, the closest surface that he could get to, she was naked and crying out with each touch of their mouth and hands. Not in a painful way, he supposed, but her need, like theirs, was out of control now. As soon as he had her stretched out on the couch, she pulled Akassa to her and undid his pants. Simeon watched as she freed his cock and took it into her mouth.

There was no jealously watching her making love to another man's cock. It was his other half, the man that made him whole. And Simeon loved him as much as he did any of his blood brothers. He knew that as much as he wanted her, so did Akassa. So, while they made love, he stripped down to his skin and held his cock. It was the most erotic thing he'd ever seen, watching them together.

She looked at him as she bobbed her head over Akassa. When she reached for him, wrapping her fingers around his own cock, he nearly came, but as she fisted him, sucking on Akassa, all Simeon could think about was that she was theirs, forever.

Come for me. Give me what I need more than my next breath, Simeon. He didn't want to, but her voice had been so smooth, her hand so firm on him that he felt his climax take him. His cum sprayed over her face and breasts, and when she pulled from Akassa's cock, he joined him in marking their mate.

His cum touched her in places Simeon's had, but more so as he was closer. They had marked her, made her theirs, but it wasn't enough. They needed more, and so did she.

"I need you." Simeon pulled her from the couch and guided her to lie back on the couch and open her legs. "I don't know if I want to eat you more than I want to fuck you right now."

"Eat me." Leaning down to her pussy, he licked her from gate to clit, then took the tiny nubbin into his mouth and suckled hard. Even as she cried out that she was coming, he slid his finger into her tightness and fucked her with it. "More. I need so much more."

Simeon couldn't have stopped even if she begged him to. Tasting her release, the way her pussy seemed to flow wet for him, he ate her like she was a Thanksgiving feast and he'd never get enough. When she cried out again, he looked up her body to see Akassa making a meal of her breasts, suckling at one then the other, leaving small bite marks behind with each taste. Bryn came twice more then, just from their hands and mouth. Simeon knew for as long as he lived, he'd see her this way, covered in their seed and crying out for more.

She came four times, each time more powerful than the last, he'd bet. The way she held them to her, begging one minute for more and the next for them to stop, she'd had too much. But they weren't finished...he wasn't sure that they'd ever be finished with her. But it was time to move this to a bigger area, the bedroom.

She was ahead of them as they walked there, not allowing either of them to touch her as she moved. He thought it was funny, really. Bryn's body was covered in small bite marks, their cum, and she was saving the rest for the bed. There, he knew, they'd make her theirs on a whole new level, and he was looking forward to it more than he was his next breath.

"I don't think this is going to work." He felt his heart stop in his chest when she said that. "I mean, you guys are both very hard and I'm just me. How does this work?"

He nearly leapt on her to show her. But instead, he had her lay on the bed in the middle, and he and Akassa on either side of her. As they started over, touching her, relaxing her, Akassa told her what they were going to do to her.

"We're going to make you come so many times just to get you relaxed." She told him that wasn't going to work. "Oh, you doubt us? Then I guess we'll have to prove you wrong. After that, I'm going to watch you get fucked by Simeon. He's going to be gentle with you, making you realize that he's in love with you as much as I am. Then I'm going to take you, hard and fast, fucking your pretty pussy until you scream out my name as you come."

Simeon wanted to take her now, have her beneath him like Akassa said, but the more he touched her the tenser she became, and when she climaxed, screaming out his name and Akassa's, he rolled her to her back and moved over her.

She was sobbing now, her body so hard with need that he knew that as soon as he entered her, took her, she was going to hurt them both. Akassa took her breast into his mouth, his fingers sliding to her pussy and into her. When she came again, Akassa moved his hand and Simeon entered her quick and hard. And waited.

Her scream this time was of pain. He didn't move but Akassa kissed her, comforted her while he felt sweat roll down his back. Simeon couldn't have moved even if he wanted; she was strangling his cock so tightly that he feared for permanent injury. When she moved, her hips just adjusting herself into a better position, he moaned.

"Christ, you're beautiful." The grin she gave him made him think she knew just what she was doing. "Move again like that and I'm not going to wait any longer. As it is now, I'm having a hard time, harder than you think, just waiting until you're ready for us."

"You mean like this." Akassa laughed and she moaned again when Simeon filled her deeper. "Oh yes. That's much better. Do it again."

"So demanding." She nodded and bowed up from the bed when he moved again. This time he laid over her, taking her breast into his mouth as he took her slowly, gently. "I love the way you tighten around me. The way your body milks me. Come for me, Bryn. I want to feel your climax."

They made love for as long as she'd let him. She was demanding...not that he minded, but she wanted relief and so did he. Knowing that he was going to have her in his life forever, Simeon let her have her release and he did as well.

It was glorious. Spectacular. He saw stars and diamonds. There was even a moment, a tiny one, when he was sure that he saw the castle in all its glory. Even as he dropped over her, his body spent, she reached for Akassa. Simeon watched the two of them while he rested.

Akassa did indeed take her hard. He looked as if he were ramming nails into the floor. As she came again and again, Simeon fisted his own cock and knew that when they came again, he was going to as well. It was the most amazing thing he'd ever realized, having a mate that was this special to them both.

Chapter 6

Gideon walked around the castle three times. No easy feat either, considering that it was about a football field across in the front and about half that shoved back up against the mountain behind it. He could see that something was different, he just didn't know what it was. So, he was standing in front of the thing when he was joined by three of his brothers.

"What did you do?" He looked over at Asher when he spoke. "I mean, it's been played with, don't you think?"

"Played with? It's a fucking rock building, Asher, not some kid's toy blocks. I think that playing with it is out of the question. But there is something different. I just can't put my finger on it." Asher nodded and asked Elam and Jed if they knew what it was. "I thought it was the windows that are now in, but that's not it either. It's something big."

The women joined them…all seven of them, including his mom. And then before they were there very long, the rest of the family showed up. It was as if someone had set up a time for them to meet, and there they all were. Everyone stared at the castle as if they too were wondering what was different. He didn't want to ask the question again, but left it to Elam. He said that something was off.

"Off good, or off bad?" Elam shrugged, and when Bryn laughed, he wondered what he'd done now. She was a little hard to get to know, he'd realized. Always so quiet and on the ready. Like she was ready to kill anything that touched her. He asked her what she saw.

"It's done." No, that wasn't it, so he looked again. "Yes, it is. It's done to the point where it can be. The magic has done all that it can for it. So the rest is up to us. I'm sure that the book will be readable now. Try it."

"Book?" Gideon turned to Asher. "Do you have it on you? I mean, if this is the time we do this, then I'd very much like to get it over with. Having this thing done will do wonders for my back and sleeping." They all laughed. Any one of them could lift up a stone the size of a car, but he understood what he meant. Done would be good.

"I don't carry around old books, Gideon, but I can go back for it. Just don't do anything until I come back." What Asher expected them to do without him was beyond him, but they all stood around and waited. When he returned, he looked a little freaked out and they asked him about it. Asher said that the book was still blank, but they had visitors.

"What sort of visitors? You know, I'm mighty sick of people just showing up unannounced like this. You'd think we was running a show here or something." Mom hushed Dad and turned to Asher. "Well, it is mighty hard to have a quiet moment or two with your loved ones when they keep popping up like one of them kid toys."

"Who is it, son? No one we know, I'm guessing." He

shook his head and handed the book to Essie. "The book isn't working, you said? That's all right. We'll get it to work. Tell us about the people."

"No, not yet. I wasn't sure that we all had to be together when we tried it, but I guess that's not it. About the visitors, they're in town. Not here yet. They're planning a meeting. And while Victor, the hotel manager, doesn't know exactly what they're here for, he's seen a couple of pamphlets that let him believe that they're slayers. A big group of them, too."

"What do you want to do?" Gideon didn't like the look on Bryn's face when she spoke. It was hard and deadly. When she glanced at him, he had a feeling that, like most of the women in the family, she could read his mind. Her next words confirmed it. "I say we just let them hang themselves by coming out here. I know that Gideon thinks that they're as good as dead as far as I'm concerned. And he's right. End this shit once and for all."

"No, I didn't." He lowered his voice when his mother cleared her throat. "What I mean is, I don't want to kill the lot of them when there might be a better solution. You know, like asking them nicely to go away."

"You think that's going to work with these men?" He didn't and told her that. "Well then, why are we wasting our time in doing this when we could just go there, end them, and move on with our lives?" She looked at Asher. "I have enough men right now to finish this if you want."

"What do you mean, men?" Gideon looked around. "There isn't anyone here but us. Unless you plan on taking the faeries with you from here, but I don't think that's going to do you a bit of good. I know that they have magic and all, but to think that they can do any real harm to anyone is just...."

Well, you know, like I said, they're very tiny."

"Really? All right then, Gideon, how about we have a bet. You stand right there, and I'll show you what kind of damage my army of faeries can do." He knew that he should have turned her down, but he heard his brothers laughing and he stood where she told him. The tree behind him was strong and sturdy, and he knew if need be, he could get behind it, but as soon as the swarm came to stand beside Bryn, he realized he might have made the biggest mistake of his life. And hopefully not his last one.

The pip, what he'd heard a group of faeries were called, came at him at once. Not one of them touched him as they flew around him, and he had to close his eyes against the dizzying speed that they were moving. He felt things touch his face and arms, but nothing heavy or painful. When the buzzing stopped, he opened his eyes and looked at his family. They were staring at him as if he had a gun in his hand.

"That was scary, but I think I've proven my point, don't you think?" They were still staring at him oddly, and he finally had enough. "What are you staring at? I'm not harmed, just as I said I'd not be." Gladly too.

"Come here and look." Gideon moved from the tree toward Asher when he waved him over. "Just don't make any sudden moves, all right? I don't know how safe that is around you."

"What are you talking about?" He was facing Asher when he took his shoulders in his hand and turned him. When he did, he fell on his ass and stared at what they'd done. "Christ. What the fuck?"

"Gideon. Your language, please." He nodded at his mom, but continued to stare at what was left of the tree. "It's a good likeness of you, don't you think?"

The tree was gone, or at least most of it was, but what was left was a carving of him. Not just a crude one, but an exact replica of him. Even his boots, which he'd not tied, were there, and his scruffy hair. All it needed to have was color and he was sure that someone would be hard pressed to tell the difference. Christ, they'd done that, with him standing there, in a matter of seconds, and he'd not been touched once. He looked at Bryn.

"They might have gotten a little zealous in doing this for you, but as you can see, they're very good at carving out a solid piece of wood when they're playing around. Can you imagine what they'd do with a human being? One that would try and harm anyone here? Or for that matter, anyone not human? They're the best there is, Gideon, and they are very tiny, as you said." She laughed again. "Why don't you stand still again, and we can show everyone what else they can do to one. You don't mind being an example, do you, Gideon?"

"I don't like you." They all laughed, but he wasn't sure that anyone actually thought this was funny. It was fucking scary, is what it was. "You trained them to do this? For sport?"

"No, I trained them to kill, but they had to hone their skills at it. They're small, as you've noticed, and they can be knocked away very easily. What they did here, it was the best way to show you that they're strong. In a matter of seconds, they can kill a full-grown man, and not one of them will be harmed. They work as a single unit, and as you can see, they're huge in number, so they'd be bigger than any dragon here should they wish to be."

Tinsel came to land on his shoulder and Gideon let him. He'd been hanging out with him since they'd arrived. Bryn had quit him, and while he wasn't entirely sure what that meant, the little brownie had been heartbroken. He cried about his stupidity every day.

"Hello." Gideon looked at Anthony when he simply appeared. "My goodness, to see you all here together makes me think that Eve and I did a good job in this. How are you, Brynhilde?"

"Mad at you still, so don't go getting all mushy with me. You misled me in having me come here, and you know it." He grinned and nodded. "And he has the book, fat lot of good it's done him. The magic isn't working for us. If there was any in the first place. How could you do this to me? To them?"

"Oh, but it has. Look at the castle. It's done." She pointed out that it was nearly done before she arrived. "Yes, but now the magic is working its way through the stone. Soon it will be made of the most impregnable rocks ever made. All thanks to you doing what I asked of you. And you didn't make it easy on me, either. The way you'd just lie there, waiting for something to befall you. I had a headache for hours after."

No one mentioned that he'd died shortly after that...no more than a couple of days, as a matter of fact. Gideon was helped to his feet, and he looked at the carving again. To think that he'd been standing there when they'd done it. Turning to the family, he listened to what was being said. Or in this case, what was being argued over. It would never be boring with his family, he thought.

"So that's why I brought the book here? So that the castle, that's made of stone, can be stronger? That's it?" He rubbed his head, something she'd seen him to several times that night she'd spoken to him. She was glad, Gideon realized, that she was frustrating the poor king. "And now what do we do? Sit inside and let the slayers come and slaughter the dragons?"

"You know, I think I liked you better when you were a bit more subservient. No, we do not just sit back and wait for that. You'll take care of them, all of you will, and once you do, this will be finished once and for all." She asked him how that was going to happen. "You do have to kill them."

"No." His mom moved toward the king. "No more killing, please. Being dead and with the dead has taught me a few things. We should talk to them. See if we can work something out. You know, like a compromise or something. Surely we could do that rather than just have a bloodbath. Something needs to be done, I know this, but death is so.... Please?"

"I'm afraid these men are on a path much like the one that the villagers were all those years ago, young Sally. They have it in their heads not just to kill every dragon that has gathered here, but all of you as well. And they're being fueled by a single man, a man that I have not seen in a great many years." Gideon asked him who. "Wilson. I'm not sure if he's using a last name as is the custom now, but he is one of the original members of the slayers from all those years ago."

"Wait. One of the original members? You mean, he's like us? An immortal?" Anthony shook his head. "Then I don't understand. How could he be one of them from all that time ago?"

"He's an immortal, but he can be killed. You cannot, not since Brynhilde joined the family. Iron can kill him, as well as slicing his head from his body. He can sustain injuries, as well as bleed to death. And before you ask, yes, he's the one that has been moving people into your way all along. I only just found out about it when I was awakened. He's even behind Helena and her fumbling around. Not the fumbling part, but you understand. Getting others to do his work has always been his way of doing things. And in this, he's failed at every attempt. And I for one would like to see him finished." Gideon asked why he was doing this now and not before. "You weren't as strong as you are now. There is literally no one out there, not even a whole group, that can take you down. Not anymore. Not that he won't try. He's always been someone that can't take no for an answer. But you must kill him, and some of his flock. It's the only way to disband them completely. A show of force...it's got to be that way so that others will realize that it's not worth the death count."

"I don't know why it should matter. I mean, as you said, we're all immortal now. There isn't any way for him to kill us." Anthony said nothing, but he could tell he was frustrated with their mom. "Why can't we just try and talk to them? I mean, wouldn't it be better that way? No more bloodshed?"

"Several hundred years from now, they'll return if we don't do this now. And when they do, you will have to stand by and watch the ruination of your family; the other dragons here, as well as the ones coming, will begin to die off too because there will be no children born to them. They'll not be able to kill your loved ones, not with the magic that they now have, but they can hide them in a way that they shan't be found. Their bodies will be alive, their minds as well, but they will be under the dirt and water so that no one can find them. And no one will even know how to look for them or where. The magic of the land, it depends on the dragons. When they're gone, so will be the magic. And he will leave you here, you and Jacob, to be the last of your kind, to live out the rest of your days, forever. There will be no dragons, no magic here, except the part that keeps your hearts beating...

your broken hearts, that is." Mom looked at all of them, then back at Anthony as he continued. "Neither Eve nor I wish for that to happen to the nicest, kindest family that we have ever met. Without the two of you and your kindness, none of us would be here. The dragons would have nowhere to have hidden. There would be no children born to them. All because of the two of you. And he knows this. It's why his plan is to leave you here with nothing. Because to his way of thinking, you are nothing."

"They'll do this? They'll come anyway?" Anthony nodded at Gideon when he asked. "But if we do this, this showing of our force, they'll leave us alone? All slayers will go away and never bother us or the dragons again? How can you be so sure about something so permanent? I mean, it's not that I don't believe you, but how can you know?"

"Never would they bother you again. And it will happen because the man who will have been there, forever, will be dead. He will no longer be pushing people into doing his work. There will be no more of his magic being used to manipulate others into trying to kill you. His body will become dust and you'll be free of him. As I said, forever." Anthony looked at Mom. "You must allow them to end this, Sally. If they don't, all that you've lived for, every person's life that you've touched and loved, will be dead. And you will be alone again. It is a fate that I would not wish on anyone, but especially you and Jacob."

Gideon wasn't sure what she was going to do. Mom looked like she was hurting from the things that she'd been told. And he was too. To have come all this way, to have found such happiness here with his love and family, to see it all for nothing, hurt his heart so badly.

"Kill them." Anthony told Mom that he was sorry for this. "So am I, my lord, but I won't have this family suffer again. And I won't lose them again, not like this. This is something that I have dreaded my entire life, the ending of something so wonderful. And if it takes the killing of a few, I hate it, but I want it to end. Now. Today if we can."

Anthony nodded and moved to stand next to Asher. As they spoke quietly, Mom turned to him and his other brothers. He saw how much this was costing her—what it took from her to condone murder—but she patted him on the cheek then walked away. He ached for her, but knew that this was the only way they'd all be safe. Then she went back the way she'd come, toward home.

Gideon loved his mom more in that moment than he had at any other time in his life. She was the bravest woman he knew, and a warrior. Mom, his mom, would keep them all safe, no matter what it took. He'd known that, he supposed, but right now he felt it all the way through his heart. His mom was as brave and as strong as any warrior that had ever come to the battlefield.

~~~

Wilson looked at the single book he'd been able to gather. Not that it did him much good. The language that it had been written in had been dead longer than some dragons had been. Now that he was close to getting all that he wanted more than anything, things weren't going his way. And he had a feeling that his book, the one that had been stolen from him all those decades ago, was now in the very hands that could use it. The new king would be able to destroy him. And he wasn't going to let that happen if he could help it.

"Sir? There's a call for you." He asked his man who it

was. "They wouldn't tell me, sir. And when I explained that I'd not put the call through for him, he just laughed and said to tell you that the new king wished to speak to him."

His balls, something that he'd not had much use for over the last few centuries, tightened to his body. The king? The new king had found him? Not possible. He cleared his throat and tried to think how that had been possible, and asked Pearson what he'd said. He pulled out a sheet of paper, saying that he'd told him to write it down.

"He claimed that his name was Asher, named for the fallen castle that you destroyed. That his middle name is Anthony, for the greatest king that ever reigned. And that his parents are Jacob and Sally, friends of the kingdom and all that lived there." Pearson looked at him. "He said that he is brother to the hatchlings that you knew nothing of. That there are six of them, children of the king and queen."

"Not possible." Pearson said nothing but stared at him, as if he wasn't going to disagree verbally but knew it to be true. "And he's on the phone? Right now, awaiting me to talk to him? Why would he be calling me? I don't want to...did you tell him my name, perchance?"

"No, sir, I'd not do that, but he seemed to know not only who you were, but why you were here. He said that it would behoove you to speak to him, that you might live longer." Pearson looked confused. "Are you not an immortal, sir?"

"I am." He stood up and began to pace. Really to work off some of his frustrations. He would have to talk to the man, if for no other reason than to see if even a small portion of what he was thinking was going on. Like, how did Asher know of him? Where had he been all these years? What did he mean, he might live longer? He was immortal, the same as the king was. "Send his call to here. I'll see what he has to say for himself. And Pearson, make sure you see if what he says is true, that there are other dragons of the old king."

After he was left alone, he went to sit at his desk. He wasn't sure he wanted to talk to this person, but he needed to find out what he knew. And that, he figured, was the only way to kill him. Picking up the phone when it beeped, he waited for the man to speak. Only an idiot would give in and speak first as far as he was concerned.

"Hello, Wilson. We weren't sure that was what you went by anymore, being that it's your true name. How are you? Dying, I hope." The laugher grated on his nerves, so much so that he nearly hung up. "Oh, don't do that. Hanging up on me might make it so I think you don't like me. While you will learn to hate me, right now, you need me."

"And why is it you think I care? You never said your name, by the way." Asher told him that he knew it, he'd given it to his man. "So? I've forgotten. Meaningless people, I tend to forget their names. I will forget yours too, as soon as this call is disconnected. And you are meaningless to me, Asher the new king, and you'll soon be dead too."

"You're going to remember me. It might well be the last name you utter before I crush you." He heard the small laughter, and Wilson knew that he was being played with. "I promised my mom that I'd ask you to stop this nonsense and leave us alone. She has it in her head that you're not going to come here and make it so we have to kill you. That we can work something out. I tried to tell her that you were stupid as well as stubborn in thinking that you could come out on top, but a promise to my mom is important, don't you think? How about yours? Did you ever make one to her and not follow through on it?"

Wilson decided to not answer the questions about his mother and unkept promises. He'd killed her long ago. Or he'd watched her being killed. Pitting brother against brother had been the only way to make the king of his time dead. And if his own family had fallen too, well, so be it.

"Work out what? How I'm going to take over your kingdom? Or perhaps how you're going to beg me for mercy? You will, you know. All of you. I might be persuaded to leave your dear mother alone, but it's doubtful." Wilson laughed then. "Am I to assume that you've been reading up on the books about me? I have been around longer than you have. And in that time, I've learned a trick or two about making dragons and humans suffer when I want."

"Have you? Doubtful you'll do much to us. And I'm to tell you that Brynhilde said hi. I wasn't aware that you knew my sister-in-law until today." Wilson stood up, then sat again. Brynhilde? She was alive? "She said that you and her crossed paths some time ago, and that she owes you for the death of her family. I don't think she means that in a good way. She said that you were the last one she needs to kill for their deaths. And she will too, just so you know. I think she'll take great pleasure in making you suffer as well."

"Then she should have done what she'd been told." He thought of the night she'd refused his order to murder the dragon he'd found. And her words still, to this day, haunted him like none other. "Am I supposed to believe that you have let her become a part of your family, young Asher? That is a fatal mistake on your part. She's not to be trusted. The things that I could tell you about her would curl your toes, as the saying goes. Perhaps before I kill you, I could have a nice sit

111

down with you. It would be a sharing of horror stories, so to speak."

"Thank you, but no. I know her well too. Funny, she said the same about you, about not to be trusted. She also said that you're a mean bastard that she wants the pleasure of killing." He pointed out that she couldn't do that. Not ever. "Can't she? I think you should check on that, Wilson. With me being the king, I can pretty much let her do whatever she wishes, including ending your life. She was claimed by King Anthony, and I have her services now as well."

Was that true? He didn't think so, but then, he had no idea. While he knew a great deal about the dragons, how they were to be killed and then sold off, he hadn't a single idea about what the faerie warrior could or couldn't do. She was a commodity, not a person anyway.

"I tell you what, young Asher, you take your hold off her and I'll take her into my house. It's the least I can do for you, being that she might be spared when I come to claim everything you have." The laughter again, and Wilson had to let out a long breath before speaking. There wasn't any point in losing his temper now. "What if I promised you that she'd not kill you? I'll save that pleasure for myself."

"How kind of you." Wilson smiled. Finally, he was making some headway in this. "And as for Bryn, no, I won't release her. Not that I could anyway. Anthony holds her, not I. Oh, and before I forget, he and Eve send their condolences."

"They're dead." Asher told him he was correct. "Yet you tell me that you've spoken to them? And their condolences about what?"

"Your sister. She's gone." The line went dead, and he sat there for several seconds before he stood up and went to find

Maureen. She'd been with him since he'd taken her from his parents' burning home. Going to her room, he stood there as he watched her frail body swing back and forth on the rope that was wrapped like a necklace around her pretty neck. She was dead, he knew this even before he realized her delicate neck was snapped.

The note was handed to him. He didn't know who had come to help him, but when he looked up, her body had been cut from the beam and now lie in her bed. Going there, with the note in his hand, he thought of the couple who had killed her. The king and queen dragons.

My darling brother, I have had enough. He looked down at her when he read that, and knew in his heart that she hadn't had any help from a dead king and queen. Maureen had told him several times over the last few weeks that her body was worn out, she was in constant pain and wanted to die. *We both know that I've been a drain on your life. You might not say so, but I can see it. Everyone can. So, I'm doing what you will not, ending my suffering. I love you with all that I am, but enough is enough. I've loved you with all my heart and then some. You have taken care of me through all my pains and troubles. You have been the best brother that anyone could have asked for, but I hurt, Wilson. I hurt so badly that I'm no longer able to shed tears for it. They're as dried up as my willingness to live. Please forgive me, but as I have said, I've had enough of this earth.*

He looked at her again, her badly scarred flesh. Her hair that only grew on the one side of her head. Wilson held her hand, what was left of it from the fire, and sobbed. His little sister was gone.

It didn't lessen his pain, knowing that she was at peace. Those words said to him about his parents were as meaningless then as they were now. He was alone, and his only friend and companion had taken her own life. As he sat there, holding her hand, he thought of the day that he'd figured out that King Anthony had been a dragon.

His house has been set to flames, and the only person that could do such a thing, such devastation, had to be a dragon. The king, he had done this to him in order to show who was the bigger man. Wilson had gone to see him, the smell of burnt flesh still upon his clothing. The dragon had wanted his sister dead. The reason, if there had been one, had never been clear to him, then or now, but someone had to be blamed.

"We didn't murder your sister, Wilson. I swear this to you." He didn't believe him. What was a dragon for but to burn people to death? "The fire was started in the stove, as everyone has told you. The dragons, nor my wife and I, were not involved in their deaths. We liked her very much."

Of course, he didn't believe him. King Asher was as bad as the old king, and he'd make sure that he was just as deceased when the time came. Wilson's sister was dead now, just as surely as he'd set the rope to her neck.

"I will see you dead, and all the others that come after you. Death to all dragons. You are no king to me." He'd stormed off after his threat to Anthony, his mind plotting and planning.

Days later, he'd gone to see the witch and had convinced her to do harm to the king, telling her that they'd caused the hurt of so many. His sister had lived, thanks in part to his magic and that of the witch, but she'd been badly scarred. And Wilson's family had not helped when they turned her away when she screamed in so much pain. They paid too, he'd made sure of it.

Wilson had wanted Anthony dead, and had succeeded in making it happen. He knew that he'd have to have magic, more than the king did, and had made it his life's mission to get as much as possible. Running into the witch Helena had been the first of many things Wilson did to make his promises run true. And now it was about to come full circle. He'd kill Asher and then all the dragons, and rule the world with all the magic that would come to him.

Chapter 7

The castle looked complete, but Asher knew that it needed something more. Something from the book. As he sat there, holding onto it while looking at the massive pile of stone in front of him, he thought of his life thus far. When something snapped beside him, he looked over and saw Bryn coming toward him. Moving so that she could have a seat, he waited for her to speak.

"The castle was built with such power. I mean, the first one. And it stood for something. Something that none of those watching it being built could have ever guessed. And it's doubtful that anyone, even after it was fallen, could have known. It was strength, safety as well as hearth. None of those things were here before King Anthony came to live here." He asked what it had meant to her. "Nothing. I had no allegiances to the king nor his household. I had none to anyone unless they claimed me. And unbeknown to me, he had."

"Did you ever really have any allegiances to anyone that claimed you?" She thought about it, but in the end said that

117

she had not. "What about to us? As a family, not a warrior. Do you feel anything toward us? Or Simeon and Akassa?"

"I don't love them, if that's what you're asking me. I don't have much in the way of heart left, Asher. It's been used up, on battlefields. Blood that was shed for no more a reason than greed. People, human or otherwise, will eventually show their true colors. Not here. For some reason, I think that you are just what you say you are. And that is a rarity, even to me." He nodded. There wasn't much he could say to her to convince her that Simeon and Akassa loved her...Asher knew that they told her daily that they did. "Did you know that this castle is magical? I don't mean the stuff that you have put into it, nor the things that the king has given it, but it has a bit more."

"Like what?" She told him to watch the walls when she walked to it, pulling her sword from her back. "What are you going to do?"

He watched her as she slashed her sword toward the stone. Asher wasn't sure what she'd done and asked her to do it again. This time he stood near her as she slashed out, and couldn't believe what he saw.

"Did you do that?" She smiled and told him that she had not. Once more he asked her to try and harm the stone, and he was amazed when the stone moved, slicing itself open as her blade came close to it so that she'd not touch it. "What else can it do? I'm assuming that there is more. Christ, it's saving itself from harm. That is.... Well fuck, that's amazing. Show me. I need to see it."

"All right. It can hide itself and those that are within. I think that is one of the things that the book brought to it." He told her that he couldn't see the words yet. "Yes, I've been thinking on that as well."

They made their way back to the seat that had been put in some time ago. He didn't press her. He'd learned that none of the women liked to be hounded with questions, especially this one. She would answer you in time, and hurrying her along wasn't going to get her to do it any faster. It might well piss her off, and he didn't want to do that. He was enjoying just sitting with her in the sunlight. He bided his time while watching a group of dragons play in the field beyond.

He'd been informed just yesterday that all the dragons that could come were here. There were a few, less than a dozen, that didn't want to travel. Or couldn't. Some were very old and still banged up from years of attacks. The rest... well, he'd heard that they didn't believe they could be any safer here than where they currently were, and decided to chance it.

Also, there were hatchlings being born now. Several a day, as a matter of fact. Not that they'd be overrun by newborns. Hatchlings were only born to dragons every several thousand years. He supposed because they were so large that having one every few months would not only drain the parents, but the land and earth as well. Asher supposed it was a balancing act in that way. When he looked back at Bryn, she spoke.

"I don't love them. I've thought about it, but there isn't anything in my heart for either of them. I'm sorry about that. They're wonderful men and are very kind to me, but I don't love them as I think I'm supposed to." He asked her why she thought that. "Because I don't complete the circle. I don't love them, not like you guys do each other, and that's why neither the magic for the book nor the castle works. Because my heart is too hard for it to be opened. I don't know if it ever will, either."

"That makes sense, I suppose." He thought that she might *say* she didn't love them, but he could see the way they looked at her and her at them. There was something there, a spark, he thought. "What if you're right? I mean, what do you suppose could be holding you back? Not that I want you to do something that you're not feeling, but how is it you're so sure that there isn't love there?"

"I don't hate them, if that's what you're saying." He said that it wasn't. He was just asking to be sure. "I don't feel anything overwhelming for them. I know that they love me, they tell me that all the time, but I don't think I'm capable of loving them. I'm hardened, as I said. I've seen too much, Asher. Done more than most in the name of greed...not mine, but that of someone else, and even love. That is far worse than greed."

"People say that they're in love a great deal. It has become so common for people to say it to someone that it's as automatic as asking how they're feeling, or about the weather." She leaned back on the stone bench he was sitting on as he continued. "I'm glad that you're taking your time with this. Being honest. You've told them, haven't you? Let them know how you feel?"

"I have. I don't think they believe me." He could see that as well, them telling her that she'd fall in love with them someday. Asher was sure that she would, but it would take some time. "The man, Wilson. You do know that he was my master at one time, don't you?"

"Yes, you told me. He's also the one that killed your family. I don't know why, but I had assumed that you'd taken care of him. It's none of my business, but why haven't you?"

She didn't answer him. "Is that why you can't love, Bryn?"

"Some of it, I think, but as I said, it's what I do, what I've seen." Asher asked her if she'd seen any goodness. "Yes. Not as much as the death and other things, but yes, there was goodness as well. And the reason that I never took care of him, as you said, was because I thought him dead. Along with his household. I killed them all. Killed them in ways that even as old as I am, it sickens me to think that I went that far. I will end him as he did my family. And he will suffer."

"We, too, have seen a great deal. All of us…not for as long as you, but we've been around a long time. And as you said, greed is there. Love is thrown around like it's a curse word too, at times. But all I need to do is look at my children, and those of the others, and I know that there is happiness out there. Love too, when I see my wife. And my parents. I'm not saying that you can get over this. No, it's not that…I do hurt for your loss in that."

"It didn't feel like loss until now. Not when I see so much love around me. Everyday." He had a feeling that there was hurt because deep down, she loved Simeon and Akassa, but was, like him at first, afraid to admit it. "Wilson is going to die. I'm going to make sure of it. And I would like to ask a favor of you. I don't want your mom to know just how he dies."

"You're going to make him suffer badly?" She nodded at him. "Good. I'd like to say that it won't make a difference to you if you do this or not, that it won't bring them back, but I think that he needs to suffer. Because as much as it pains me to say this, I'm betting that he's done far worse to other families, and that you will do the best job of it. You frighten even me at times."

121

She laughed. It was a belly laugh, as if she'd been caught unawares of something he'd said. When she stood up and bowed before him, he stood as well. This was something that he hadn't expected either, and waited for her to say the words.

"I, Brynhilde, last warrior faerie of the kingdom of Anthony and Eve, dragon lords of old, hereby pledge myself and my sword to Asher Anthony Benson, King of the Dragons, lord of the castle." He put out his hand and she removed her sword. It was the first one he'd held in a great many years, and knew that this one was the best he'd ever handled.

"I, Asher Anthony Benson, King of the Dragons, lord of the castle, hereby grant Brynhilde, last warrior faerie of the kingdom, complete freedom." She looked up at him and he winked. "I also grant her the ability to choose who she fights for; her sword shall be her own forevermore."

Touching her sword to her shoulders, nicking the flesh there to make his mark, Asher felt the ground beneath him tremble and saw the trees shake. Anthony appeared, along with his wife. Others too…some of them dead, others as alive as him. But when his own family arrived the ground moved again, and he knew that this was what the castle had been waiting for. Not love from the woman before him, but her freedom to do as she pleased.

When she stood up, her magic filled the area around them, engulfing them both in it. Her wings spread out, longer, more colorful than before. No longer were they just random bits of color, but art filled them. The castle, dragons, and swords were there, as well as forests and other creatures that dwelled within. It was as if they too had a story to tell, and it was there for anyone to see.

As her hands rose above her head, he saw dragons form

in them, bright with color. As they shaped, they moved to her body, filling in spaces where markings hadn't been before. Her sigil changed, becoming a dragon like none he'd ever seen before.

He was large, spanning her body like it was becoming a part of her. Which, in a way, he supposed that it was. The wings on it spread out, and his head, it seemed to Asher, bowed to him. And all the while, he could see changes to the rest of her body. She was stronger, larger than life in her magic.

When she looked at him, her eyes were green like the grasses in the spring. Her hair, usually red, was now a shade so bright, so wonderfully full and rich, that he wanted to run his fingers through it to see if it was as soft and as hot as it looked.

When she evolved — it was the only thing he could think of to call what had just happened — she went to her knees, and Asher did the same. He was exhausted; his body ached with the newfound magic. And as he knelt there, he knew that whatever she'd just done, they had all shared in it, as his family was staggering to their own knees.

"Are you all right?" He nodded at Essie. "Good, because I'm not. What the hell was that? It felt like the earth moved."

"I think it did." He stood again, this time holding onto the trees or whatever else was close enough for him to touch and hang onto. Reaching for the book, he wasn't surprised to find it was full of pictures, words that were written by a great hand. Looking at Anthony, he smiled. "You knew this would happen?"

"No. I thought perhaps, as she did, that it would be love. And in a way, I think that is what it was. Your love for her and releasing her was nothing I would have anticipated, but I surely do think it was the perfect thing for you to do." Anthony pulled Eve to him. "We're not for this world any longer. Our tasks are complete. You no longer need us or our guidance. Not that you needed much of it anyway. I'm very proud of you, Asher, king of dragons. More than I could have ever been, I think."

"No, you can't leave us. We.... We're not finished here. We have so much to learn from the two of you." Anthony shook his head and smiled at him. It was sad and painful, the look he gave him, and Asher wanted to grab him and hold him to him. "Please, don't leave. We've only just gotten to know you."

"Yes, and it was a great pleasure, as well as an unexpected one, to see you all together. But as our time here was never meant to be, it is something we must correct. You will be fine, all of you will now." Asher asked him about the slayers. "Asher, look around you. Do you think that anyone could breach this family? Do you think anyone in their right mind would come here and try to harm you? Nay, they will not. You are as safe here as I wish we were so long ago. But then, things might have turned out differently, and that would have been equally as sad. We must go."

As they faded out, he watched the rest of the family tell them goodbye, but he was the only one that had begged them to stay. His family understood better than him, he supposed, that they were only guests in this world, and it was time to let go. Asher wasn't sure he could do this without their help. He looked at Simeon when he stood beside him.

"You're going to be fine." He nodded, a lump in his throat that made it hard to swallow. "You're going to be a great leader, king, and brother. Not that you weren't before, but now you'll be better. We'll all be just fine now. I know it."

He hoped so, he surely did, because while Wilson couldn't kill them, he could expose them to all sorts of trouble. And that, more than anything, was what worried him. He didn't want people coming around just to have a look at dragons. There would be no peace for them if Wilson did that.

~~~

Simeon moved on the bed and felt the warmth of Bryn beside him. She'd been so quiet since yesterday that he simply wrapped her into his arms and held her. When she moved her body closer to his, he kissed her bare shoulder and held her.

"I'm free." He kissed her again rather than speaking. Her voice was so quiet that he didn't want to break the silence of the morning either. "I've never been free before. I feel like I want to run through the woods screaming it to the top of the mountains."

"I'm sure that everyone would understand." She giggled and turned to her back to look at him. Akassa woke too, and leaned on his elbow to watch them as well. "I was wondering if you were going to help us today or work on your lessons for Mark. He's getting very good with his sword."

"He is, but no, not today. We're moving Essie and the rest into the castle today." He smiled, thinking that this was going to be the most fun that he'd had moving furniture for someone. "But before then, I was wondering if you'd like to have sex with me. The two of you."

"Yes, always." Simeon laughed at Akassa and his immediate answer. "Sorry, but I just can't seem to get enough of you. Not just for sex, but everything about you."

"I like the way I feel when you guys are with me as well.

125

And like you, it's not just the sex, though that is amazing, but the company too." Simeon leaned over her and kissed her nipple, and moaned when the tiny tip hardened in his mouth. "More. I need a great deal more."

"Gladly." She was naked from last night. They all were. So, rolling over her to settle between her thighs was easy. Akassa took her breasts in his mouth, nibbling on one then the other, as Simeon slid deep inside of her. It was wonderful to have her so hot and ready for him, and he got the biggest thrill in watching her enjoy Akassa too.

Simeon took her slowly. He loved the way her face showed how she was feeling, how her body tightened around his when Akassa bit just a little too hard. Even as she cried out that she was coming, he knew that she was far from finished. That she'd enjoy them for the rest of the day should they want to.

Simeon made love to her body. He touched her where he could reach, kissing flesh that was there for the taking. Bryn was theirs, forever, and someday he knew that she'd love them as much as they did her. After he came, filling her body with his own, he moved away from her and stood near the bed. Watching Akassa make love to her was as fulfilling as it had been for him, but he had something to do, and left the bedroom to them.

Winter had returned for a few days, but today it was as pretty as a spring day. He moved to the side of their home, his focus on the one thing that he knew would complete their family. Tinsel was waiting for him, as if he'd known that he was going to come there at this time. He supposed the little man had, in a way.

"You've done it?" Tinsel nodded and bowed to him.

"She's either going to be very happy with us, or extremely upset. I'm hoping for the first, how about you?"

"I have the same hopes, my lord." He moved to sit upon his shoulder. "I talked with Lord Asher and the others. He thinks this a fine idea you have."

"You had, Tinsel. This was your idea more than mine. I'm glad to have been a part of it, but this is wholly your idea. Unless it goes south, then I'll take equal blame. And she deserves this, I think." Tinsel said he thought she did as well. "Akassa is going to bring her down in a bit. We're having breakfast together in the new kitchen at the castle, and then setting to work. You're sure that this will do the same as the other?"

"Yes, my lord. I spoke with Lord Anthony and his lady when they returned to the caves. He gave it his blessings, and told me to have it cleaned by the trolls. They're a mean lot when provoked, and sometimes even when in the best of humor. But they told me they'd be honored with such a task." Simeon couldn't wait to see it. "I have had it delivered to the home of Asher. That way it would be safe for you."

He headed there now, and was glad that Asher was up and ready for him. The cloth bag was huge, and the colors of it the same as the flags that now waved in the wind above the castle. He nodded once, telling him that things were ready for them when he was. Simeon said he was headed to the castle now to set it up.

The staff was setting up the tables when he entered. Not only were there enough chairs for them all to sit round the large round table, but chairs for the babies had been brought in as well. It was going to be a family thing, them getting together once a week, more if they could make it. But this room would be reserved for family only. No one else would be invited here unless they all agreed to it. And Simeon thought it a good way to begin their new lives.

The family was the first to arrive. They were mingling around, waiting for Akassa and Bryn to show up. He'd had two cups of tea and a Danish, he'd been so nervous. But when he saw her, his love, he was blown away by her beauty.

"I thought we'd be late." She flushed when Akassa said he'd tried to make them all late. "What I meant was, I thought everyone would have started by now."

"No, we were waiting on you." She looked around, and he knew that his family had lined up behind him. Turning slightly, he could see that Asher, Kiaran, as well as Essie had made this official; they were all wearing their crowns. He stepped to Bryn's side after giving her a quick kiss. Asher cleared his throat.

"I've never done this before, so I practiced, and read up on how it was to be." Bryn asked him what he was supposed to be doing. "Hush and let me do this the proper way. Brynhilde Benson, faerie warrior and family member to us all, I give to you this sword with the blessings of everyone present and some that are not. Anthony and Eve were sad not to be here, but they have blessed theirs for you."

"I can't take that." She took a step back from the sword and looked at him. "Do you have any idea who this belongs to? I can't take this. I'm...well, I'm not worthy of it."

"Yes, you are." Asher looked at Simeon as he continued. "I'm the one that decides who is worthy or not. And I say you are. Anyway, here."

Anthony's sword, the one that they'd found near his body, was shoved at Bryn. The look on her face when she took it was something that would make him smile forever. Shock wasn't even a good word to describe her reaction.

The sword was beautiful. The gleam on it was enough to make the room light up, and the markings on it, some of them older than she was, were brighter with it in her hands. As she held it in her right hand, Simeon stepped back to give her room when she began swinging it around.

It was poetry, the way the sword seemed to become a part of her, an extension of her body, just as she had told Mark not long ago. She cut through the air and the sword sung with it. As she worked with it, getting to know the feel of it, something began to take shape around the pummel.

The metal formed around her hand, then her wrist. The more she worked with it, stabbing out, lifting up and around, he could see that not only was the blade becoming a part of her, but she a part of it as well. The colors from her wings, which were now spread out, were mingling around the blade. The scroll work became more pronounced, filling in with color now that she held it.

When she seemed satisfied with it, the way it worked, the colors that were there, she slid the long sword to her back and it blended into the place where her other sword had been, now as much a part of her as her skin. Simeon supposed, in a way, it was her skin.

"How did you get those marks? The ones that are weapons and such?" Simeon had wanted to ask her that for days now, but whenever she was naked so he could see them, he was distracted. He smiled at Onimia when he said he was sorry for asking.

"It's all right. I got them from the queen. The night that I went to see them, I hadn't any idea what they would want with me other than my sword. But she told me that I'd need every advantage that I could get, and gave me the sword and knife here on my thigh. Well, gave me isn't quite right. They appeared here, just after she touched me. The other things, the weapons that came around after they were both gone, just appeared. The guns have taken on several modifications over the years. The knives have changed into larger, stronger pieces. The stars at my neck and waist have changed metals for the needs too. Like for a troll that needs to be taken down, I would have different needs than for a man. And over the years I've come to not notice when something appears. I just use it when I need it."

Talk went on at the table as they were served. It was the beginning, he thought of it. A new start to all their lives. When they began to speak about Wilson and what the plan was to take care of him, Bryn reached over and took Simeon's hand in hers. At that moment, he knew they could and would come out a winner in all of this.

Chapter 8

Grief, Wilson knew, was coloring his thoughts. As his sister was laid to rest, her small body put onto the bier as his family had been so many years ago, he thought of the day they had died. How the house around them had swallowed them up and given everything to him. Magic beyond his wildest dreams. The way they had screamed when he'd had them killed. It was so good to have heard it. Even now, in this time, it made him smile.

But now, as his sister lay dead, the dragons had taken her beyond him and his love. He could and would blame them for her death, and they'd pay with their very lives. Of this, he was most certain, more certain than he had been about anything in his days. Wilson looked at the man standing next to him when he cleared his throat.

"My lord, the Bensons have sent a man with an arrangement of flowers and their condolences." He told him to toss it away. "There is a card as well. Would you care to read it?"

"No, I would not care to hear anything they have to say to me. This is on their heads, not mine. Throw it in the rubbish for all I care. I don't want anything to do with them. They killed her." His servant said nothing but stood there, waiting for him to.... Well, Wilson wasn't sure what he was waiting on, but he could see that he didn't approve of what he had said. "She's gone, Pearson. Gone, and they wish to send me their pity? I cannot stand them. They're the ones that are harboring those monsters, and now they must die."

"My lord, I have been with your family since before your parents married. I cared for you when they would not. You know that I only have your best interests at heart. Your sister was never harmed by the dragons...you have been told this numerous times. The fire started in the kitchen, from a candle left burning. You know this as well as I." Wilson stared at the mound of dirt and the flowers around Maureen. "Sir, this is not going to help you in any way. You must let this go."

"I will, as soon as they're all dead." He moved away then, back to his home. "I want everything packed up. I'm not going to be able to stay in that house any longer. Please send my things to the hotel near the Bensons."

The traveling back and forth had been a drain on him, but he'd do it all again just to be with his sister. Even though she was bedridden, they'd played chess when she was up for it. Watched movies together, and sometimes, if she was feeling well enough, he'd take her to the dock and they'd watch the water. Now he'd have no one to share things with. Willing his body to the hotel, he took the biggest room they had and laid upon the bed.

No one would bother him here. They'd not even know he was there unless he allowed them to. His magic was powerful;

he'd been crafting it for many years, just to kill the dragons. And the king and queen. He had done that, or so he'd thought. Now he'd have to kill this one on his own. This was all in the name of killing the murdering monsters that had roamed the earth as long as he had.

The phone was ringing, which should have struck him as odd, but when he reached for it, a woman appeared in his room. He didn't know her, not even vaguely. As he lifted his arms to kill her she sat down on nothing, and he realized that she wasn't actually in the room with him. Wilson leaned back on the bed and waited. He never spoke first when with people he did not know. He thought about stripping down and seeing how that went over with her, but she did speak before he could.

"Hello, Wilson. I'm Ariannona. You might not remember me, but I do you, and your sister. I'm sorry for your loss." Wilson said nothing but sat up straighter on the bed. "I'm wife to Elam Benson."

"You whore." Her laughter brought him from the bed, but it was useless to strike out at her. "What right do you have in coming here, especially now? You are no more welcome here than that so-called king of the monsters."

"I have every right to come here and warn you off. This is the final time that we will attempt this. We might not have done it at all but for Sally Benson. She wanted us to make sure that there was nothing redeeming about you. I can honestly tell her now that there's not. Because you're not going to stop this, are you?" He didn't even bother with an answer. "I see. Yes, I guess we'll have to kill you, and that'll be the end of it. All right then. I need a list of the followers you have. We need to pick out a few of them."

"For what? You think to convert them to your way of thinking? Is that what this is about?" She shook her head. "Then what reason would I have to hand over their names to you? Not that I'm going to, but you must tell me what you want the names for."

"We need to pick out ones that have no family. The ones that few will miss when they're killed. You know, ones that won't be harmed too badly when their spouses are dead." She'd said it so matter-of-factly that he was stunned into silence with it. "You see, in order to get you to see reason, which I don't see happening, we're going to have to kill a great many men. You included, in the event that I didn't make that clear, and once you're dead and enough of your followers are, the dragon slayers will be no more. Not even anyone that will remember why they were grouped together when the shit hit the fan. I so love that term, don't you? Brings out so many images that I—"

"You think to kill me? Do you know who I am? And what I am? I'm a powerful man...I've more magic than any of you." He laughed, feeling better every second speaking with her. "Go about your business, Anna. And I'll make your suffering to be less than the others for warning me."

"Powerful?" He watched her as she threw back her head in mirth. "You have nothing on us, you moron. Can you project your image to a different place? No, you cannot. Are you able to withstand iron? Stab wounds? What happens if your head is removed? If I cut you in your heart, do you have any idea what would happen? You're going to die. While I will not. Nothing you have, nothing you do, will prevent that from happening now. This path that you're on, it will lead to certain death, and that of a great many of your followers. You will be responsible for so many more than the ones you have killed in the past. Including your own parents."

"No, that's not possible. You and I, we're alike. The iron that I have, it'll kill the dragons in a way that will make them suffer for a long while." She shook her head and smiled. "What sort of trickery is this? Why are you lying to me? To try and make me move on? It will not happen. I will see all the dragons dead. As for my parents, what business is it of yours that I have killed them? It was for the best. They were cruel people. Not loving their child when she needed them most. And forever will I spout how a dragon killed her. Perhaps not then, but the death of her lays firmly at the dragons' door."

He knew that part of what she was saying was true. They could kill him. And he also was aware that iron would no longer harm them. Giving her the illusion that he was unaware, that he had no idea what sort of enhancements had been made for them, would give him an advantage over them. Not a large one, but enough that he could kill the dragons. But while they were stronger, the dragons were not he thought. No magic would come to them in their current form. And they would die. And that to him would be the greatest victory because as soon as the dragons were all gone, the king of them would die as well.

"There are a few things that you should know. A lot, actually, but I have no desire to sit here and give you an accounting of every little thing that has happened. But the moment that all dragons crossed over into the land that belongs to the Bensons, every creature became a true immortal." Wilson felt her words roll over him like hot oil tossed from the castle walls. "Also, I don't have to, but I want to make you aware that along with the magic that keeps us safe, Bryn is going to kill you. And she will make you suffer before she does."

"She cannot." He knew the rules of her kind, and she couldn't kill anyone that had owned her any more than she could kill a master that held her sword. "She is only talking out the side of her mouth. Tell her if she thinks that she can, to come to see me. Or better yet, I will see her."

"If you wish." She stood up and he did as well. That was entirely too easy. He was going to get to fight Brynhilde? If she were dead, then he'd have an almost clear shot at the dragons. "She said for you to meet her in the field where her parents were murdered. Bryn said that you'd know that place, since you were the one that did it."

"Yes, and she knows that I was well within my rights to do so." He laughed. "Tell her to bring her blade and we'll see how good she's gotten with it. But I'd also tell her that she should remember her own rules. She spouted them off to me often enough."

"You mean the one where you're not allowed to have sex with her? That rule seemed to have been your downfall. And all this time, you've never been tried for it. I wonder what the king would say if he knew? Oh wait, he does know. He knows all." Wilson pointed out that he'd not touched her. "No, you killed her family instead. I'm thinking that she'll not go easy on you when you come together."

Wilson paced his room after the woman left him. He wasn't worried. In fact, he was actually looking forward to the meeting. To have Brynhilde right where he wanted her would be just what he needed. He might not be able to order her to kill the dragons…that rule had been forced upon him enough times that he knew it by heart, but he could order her to kill the king and his family. Related or not she would do it, because as soon as he saw her, he was going to own her blade.

An hour after he had his plans all worked out, he received a missive from Brynhilde. There was no doubt that it was from her either; the knife sticking from his door was enough to let him know that she was angry. An angry warrior was one that made mistakes. It was what he was counting on.

Wilson felt good. For the first time in days, he felt like his old self. He even took a long shower, and fixed his hair so that it was just right. He wanted things to be perfect when he took her sword, because when he did, he was going to rule her. And ruling the warrior was as good as having her in his pocket. It was the turning tide, he knew it. Dressing in his finest armor, Wilson was as ready as he was ever going to be. He just needed a couple more things, then he'd have her.

Willing himself home to gather what he needed, Wilson stopped by his sister's grave again. There were flowers all around the area, some of them her favorites. Picking the prettiest rose blossom that he could find, Wilson stuck it into his armor, enough that it would be protected but still be seen by Brynhilde. He wanted her to know that she was as responsible for Maureen's death as the dragons, since she'd not killed them when he'd ordered her to all those years ago.

Wilson moved to his room at the hotel again. His thoughts were getting all messed up with memories. It took him several minutes of calling to his father to know that he hadn't just talked to him, but it was a conversation that they'd had the day he'd died. The day he'd been taken from him. It had been an argument, really, one that they never finished.

He'd begged his father to care for Maureen. To make sure that she had the best of medical attention, nursemaids around the clock. But he had refused him, telling Wilson that she was nothing more than a female, and such things should not be wasted on her. To him she'd always been a commodity, something to trade for more goods, money, or whatever else they deemed important at the time.

Rubbing his head, he sat down, then immediately stood. Things were fuzzy for him, like how he'd gotten here. Why he was here. But when it all came crashing onto him, he remembered that his little sister was gone. Grief took him to the floor, as did his memories of her.

When he woke, Wilson felt much better. His head no longer ached and he felt refreshed. Sleep hadn't been an easy thing since his sister had died, and he thought perhaps now that he was rested, he could do things. First and foremost, he had to get a meeting set up with Brynhilde. That would be the beginning of better things to come for him.

By the time he realized how hungry he was, another thing that had fled him in the recent days, he had made all the arrangements he could think of, including staying at his home. There were memories there, not all of them bad, and he wanted to remember Maureen during better times, and he would. As soon as this was finished. Gearing up for the meeting, which was in just two days, he decided to go out to dinner. Things were going well now, he knew it.

His armor was discarded now; he had no idea why he'd had it on. Things were still there for him to think on, but he wasn't sure of the order of things. Laying his head down, he could think clearly for a moment or two then it would race away. Wilson didn't know what was going on, but he blamed it squarely on the dragons. Everything that was wrong in his life, it was because of them. And he'd soon have that taken care of as well.

~~~

Bryn loved the shower in their home. The water pressure alone made her want to stay for hours in the little room, but today she had to get moving. This was going to be, hopefully, the best day of her life. She was going to be hosting a dinner, her first ever.

Coming out of the bathroom, she was greeted by not just Akassa, who had been in the bed when she'd gotten up, but Simeon too. Bryn told them to back off.

"Why? You think that we're going to muss you up? Honey, we live for that." She told Simeon that she had a lot of work to do. "So do we. Starting with getting you to drop that towel. Then after that, we're going to massage you so that you're not all tense. We're going to help you."

"You don't help me. You make me all hot and bothered, then I get nothing done for spending the day in bed with you." Akassa stood up, his beautiful naked form hard. "You're not playing fairly. I really do have a lot to do. It's tonight, you know."

"We know. And we'll help you, when we're finished." She growled at them both. "Drop the towel, Bryn. I want to see that lovely body of yours."

She held it tighter to her. Not that she didn't want to make love with these two, but she wanted to make them work for it. Like really hard. Backing away from Simeon when he moved closer to her, she told him to behave. It was as if she'd told him to do the opposite. He was coming closer all the time.

Akassa got down on his knees, his hard cock straining from his groin. She wanted to taste him, take him into her mouth and feel him fucking her that way. But he crawled

139

toward her until his face was right where he could eat her. Instead of pushing him away, like she knew that she should, Bryn cried out when he lifted the towel just enough to sip at her nether lips.

"Please don't do this. You guys make me crazy." Akassa laughed and she felt his hands rub up to her ass, then he cupped her. When he pulled her toward him, she felt the towel fall away and knew it was as good as done. They were going to take her. "All right, but you need to be quick about this. I—"

The climax took her breath away. It wasn't like the others that she'd had; powerful, yes, but this one was a quick mind-blowing one that made her need to hold on to the wall. As Akassa continued to feast on her, Simeon took her breasts into his hands and suckled at her nipples until she wanted to beg him to take more.

Akassa stood up when she was too weak to stand; as it was, she had to lean heavily against the wall or fall on her face. Simeon had moved behind her, his big body holding hers up while she got her second wind. She was between two of the most amazing men she knew, and their hard bodies, their cocks, were pressing into her in the most delicious places.

"We're both going to fuck you." She nodded at Simeon when he whispered in her ear. "At the same time. I hope you don't mind, but neither of us wants to wait."

"How will that work?" He told her to trust them. "I do, but I don't think this is going to work. If you take me to the bed, I'll suck on your cock while Akassa eats me."

Instead of doing what she suggested, she was lifted up. As soon as Simeon wrapped his arm around her waist and lifted her, Akassa lifted her legs and spread them wide. When he stepped between them and entered her, Bryn reached for him. It was just what they needed her to do.

"Now, relax." She wasn't sure she could with a cock inside of her, but when she felt Simeon at her rear, she started to tense up. "No baby, relax. This will be amazing, for all of us."

As soon as he entered her, she cried out. It wasn't as painful as she'd thought it would be, but Simeon told her that it was because of what she was. Her body would adjust to anything. As he fucked her several times, her body became less tense as her need shot up. Christ, they were going to kill her, and in the most wonderful way.

Her feet locked around Akassa and she wrapped her arms around his shoulders. They were taking turns with her...one would enter her deeply, the other would move back. She knew that this wasn't comfortable for either of them, holding her up as they were, but since it was their idea to begin with, she took as much as she could get from them. As they moved faster, their hands touching her everywhere, she knew that when she came it was going to be the best she'd ever had.

"Do you have any idea how much we love you?" Akassa kissed her throat and mouth as he spoke softly to her. "You make us whole. You've filled our hearts with everything that we never dreamed we'd have. I love you, Bryn."

They fucked her faster. Touched her so much that she wasn't able to tell who was touching her where. And all the while, her body built higher and higher to something. She held onto them, begging them for more, and when they both bit down on her neck, each of them taking a part of her, she felt a pause in her life. Her heart filled just as her body shattered.

The climax, such a tame word for how she was feeling,

didn't build up. It hit her like a bullet from a gun. Only it took all of her...hair, nails, toes, and brain. The blood in her heart stopped pumping. Her hearing seemed to have amplified by ten times ten times ten, and she could hear their hearts doing the same as hers. Even as she screamed, coming from the bottom of her feet, she could feel their cum filling her. And as the second, then a third release took her under, she held them to her, crying out her love for them as darkness detonated behind her eyelids.

When she woke, she was alone in the bed. There was a pretty box lying next to the chair, as well as a bag that was wearing a bow. Getting up, having to hold onto the wall and dresser for support, she took the bag and opened it first. Inside was a scanty bra and panty set, soaps and lotions, as well as a loofah. Bryn set it aside for the box. Reading the card that was there first, she smiled.

"You love us." She laughed a little. "I know that's no way to start a note to you, but we're so happy we almost forgot to give you this. Inside is the dress that we picked out for you, and would be honored if you'd wear it to dinner tonight. The thought of stripping it off you slowly has us both hard as stone."

Then it was signed with both their names. Going to the bathroom again, there was a second note. This one apologized for mussing her up and told her to have a good time, they were working. She turned on the hot water and brought the soap with her into the bathroom.

Taking a long soak now, she luxuriated in the scents of the soaps. The shampoo that had accompanied the other items smelled like heaven to her. Even the loofah felt almost too good on her skin, like everything about her was now overly sensitized by them.

When she was finished, dressed, and her hair up, Bryn looked in the mirror, turning this way and that. They had done a good job of picking out a dress. She had no idea why, but she'd expected something sexy, something sheer. But it wasn't, not at all.

The skirt to the dress wasn't full, nor was it tight. Slimming, she supposed, would be a good word for it. The sleeveless top didn't cover her sigils, but seemed to blend right into them. She'd been worried that it would look silly to have them showing, but she loved the overall effect of it all. The slipper like shoes were comfortable without being too girly, and she loved them too. Going down the stairs, she was happy to see that they'd dressed up as well. Suits and ties suited these men. Naked was better, of course, but they had company coming, and that would not do.

After kissing them both, she was sent to the dining room to set the table while they finished off the meal. It was later than she'd thought it was, and things were just about done. The first of her new family arrived just as she was putting the wine glasses on the table. Essie and Asher had come with their parents.

Dinner was great. They'd had roasted chicken and potatoes, a meal that sounded simple but was far from it. Sally had given them herbs that she'd gown, and there were vegetables already from the little hothouse garden that Lindsey had. There was even pie to have afterwards, warm apple with homemade ice cream. Stuffed, they all entered the living room to talk and to enjoy the company.

"Tinsel would like a word with you. Nothing wrong, but he feels that he's done you wrong and he wants to tell you how sorry he is."

She had been meaning to speak to him for days now, but there hadn't been enough time. When she met him in the kitchen, he and three other brownies were enjoying some small treats that Elbert had brought for them. She sat down with them as they were finishing up.

"I would like to tell you how very sorry I am, my lady." She nodded but said nothing. "I have asked the queen, and she is going to allow me to move on. I'll be there—"

"You most certainly will not be leaving here." He bowed before her as she stood up to pace. "I overreacted when I found out about the king and queen. And then I didn't come and find you afterwards to figure out why you'd been told about it and not me. I understand that now, but at the time I was still raw from a lot of things. You were a good friend to me, Tinsel, and I'd very much like for you to come back to me."

"My lady, I did betray you." She said that it was her that had done that to him. That she didn't consider that the king was his leader and he'd had no choice in the matter. "He said that you'd run in the opposite direction and never return. I'm not sure he wouldn't have had the right of it. Correct, my lady?"

"He was more than likely right. Even knowing that this was as inevitable as things could get, I was rude and mean to you. I'm profoundly sorry." She sat down again and noticed that the other brownies had left them. "I've interrupted your dinner time. I'm sorry. We can talk later if you wish."

"Nay, they have work to do as well. I have been to the place where the slayer is staying." She told him it was a hotel. "Yes. I keep wanting to call it a brothel, but I've been corrected on that too. Master Casdon, he is a good man. He's been helping me with my wording on things."

"I'm glad that you've made some friends. We both have been alone for far too long." He nodded and sat down. "You've changed too, haven't you?"

"Yes, when you did. It was a scary thing at first, not being with you when it happened. But as soon as I heard that you'd been given your freedom…well, I was able to put three and six together." She told him it was two and two. "No matter, I can add them both up just fine. But I was glad for you, and for me. With your freedom, it means that my work can be lessened now and I can care for you."

"Of course you can add, I'm very sorry." She gave him a sip of water off her finger. "And I hope I wasn't too hard on you, Tinsel. You've been my only true friend longer than anyone, and I dearly need you in my life again. I'm to meet with the slayer in the morning. I do hope that you'll be there with me."

"It will be my honor, my lady. Will you be killing him?" She said that she would. "Good. He needs to die. Did you know that he's trying to gather himself an army? No one will work with him, knowing that you're free and that he's going to die. I've been spreading the word about that he will pay for his crimes. I think that has kept them away as well. No matter if he had ten hundred men, he'd still be a goner. You give it to him good, my lady."

She didn't bother correcting him this time. And she hoped that Casdon didn't teach him too much. Bryn sort of liked the way he talked. It was annoying at times, trying to figure out what he was talking about, but it was fun too.

145

Chapter 9

He had an army. Not a large one, nor all that experienced, but Wilson had one that that was more than he had hoped for when he awoke this morn. Looking around the large open field where he'd agreed to meet Brynhilde, he was satisfied with the results. She would die here, close to where her family had, and that gave him a bit of happiness in his otherwise horrific life. All he could think about was that his Maureen was gone.

Today had been especially hard on him. He wanted to talk to her about what his plans were, but she was gone from him. He wanted to tell her of how he was going to celebrate with her when he was the winner, but that wasn't to be either.

So, Wilson had gone to her grave to speak to her there. However, he was distracted when he saw that the flowers had died, all of them, and he hated to see them upon her. Having his staff clean up the area, he noticed that several of them hadn't shown up, people that had worked for him for decades. He asked where they had gone. It was then that he'd been told that they'd left his service.

"Left? Just when things are about to come out better for us? How could they do that?" Pearson told him that they had primarily cared for his sister, and that their grief, like his, was too much to bear. "Oh. I understand, but I wish they had told me. I would have found something for them to do. As it is now, things might not get finished when they need to be. See that no one else leaves my house, Pearson. We're going to be entertaining soon, and everyone will be needed. We're going to have to have a large party when they're all dead, and I'm going to invite all of my friends."

The look he'd been given made him pause, but Pearson turned then. There were going to be changes soon, something that he should have done before now. His staff was getting older, and though he'd granted them immortality, he knew now that had been a mistake. He wanted fresh and new, like his home. Wilson made a mental note to take care of that as soon as he got home today. Yes, it was well past time to take care of things. Things for the better, for all of them.

When he turned and looked out over the field where her home had once been, he was surprised that Brynhilde wasn't alone. They wouldn't be able to help her, he knew that, but to have so many people there was going to mess up his plans slightly. He had told his army that if he should look as if he was losing the battle, which he didn't anticipate, they were to kill her. Wilson didn't care if people thought it was cheating. He was in this for the win, not rules. He was going to change them anyway when this was finished. Now, with all these people around, it would be harder to do. Not impossible, but much more difficult.

"Wilson, are you sure that you want to go through with

this?" He laughed, showing her that he was more than ready to kill her. "It is my duty to explain to you that I'm a true immortal. That any wound that you inflect upon me will not kill me. Also, that I have been set—"

"Yes, yes, I know what you are. As immortal as me. You'll see that I don't care about your rules or what you have to say to me." She shook her head, but he was too excited to let her speak when he had his own rules to impart. "I command that you raise your sword with me. I take you, Brynhilde, warrior faerie of old, to do my bidding as I see fit."

"It won't work." He asked her why not. "As I started to tell you, I've been freed. No man can hold me anymore. The king, who held me in his services all these years, has given me my freedom, as well as forgiven me of my past deeds."

"That's ridiculous. You were born to serve. What good is it to have you born if you can't take up your arms and fight for someone? Does he know what he has done? Not just to me, but to all mankind? No, that's not right." He looked at the men and women behind her. "I want you to kill them all. Now. Remove their heads and be done with it."

"I cannot. No, that's not right." She lifted her sword and he smiled. Finally, she was ready to do as he said. "I don't want to do as you say. I am a free person, held by no one, now or ever again. I don't have to do what you tell me, and even if I were bound, I could not."

"You can't be serious. Why the hell would anyone do such a thing? That new king? Does he have any idea what kind of repercussions this will have on the outcome of today?" He looked at the man standing in the middle. A big man, but he waved him over anyway. The one standing next to him came as well. "Are you the king that I spoke to? The one that has set her free?"

"I am. Asher Benson." Wilson nodded. "And I set her free because she has no reason to fight for anyone any longer. It's about time that she was her own person, don't you think? I mean, she should have things her way for a change. Not at the rule of —"

"No, I don't think that at all. And no one in their right mind would either. You're a moron. Do you have any idea what sort of power she has? The way that her mind works when she's held by someone? Christ, man. She's a weapon that only gets stronger as she gets older. And she is very old, so her powers would exceed any that man could ever make by machines. And her sword was there for anyone with the right amount of coin to hold." The man only crossed his arms over his massive chest. He looked at the other man. "Are you any more reasonable than he is?"

"Doubtful. In fact, I'm betting that he's the more reasonable of the two of us. With her being free, does this mean that you're going to stop this nonsense and go away and leave us to ourselves?" Wilson wondered if these people knew what a dragon could do when they were pissed off, and asked them. "Yes, I know firsthand what a dragon can do when they're mad. You should remember that yourself."

"I'm assuming that you have been watching them at play. While they destroy those around them, you've been pampering them. Giving them whatever they want. They'll turn on you. I've seen what they can do when they do." He asked if he was talking about the fire at his home. "Yes, I am. They hurt my sister, and she recently died from her wounds. The dragons did that. Anthony and Eve. They burned my house to the ground with my sister inside."

The man touched his hand to Wilson's head. It wasn't painful, but Wilson fell to the ground. Memories, old and new, ran by his closed eyes, and he saw his home burning as if it were yesterday. And when he saw his sister's body, burned nearly to death, he sobbed, thinking that she might have been better off dying then instead of suffering so much.

"You caused the fire." He looked at the man who had touched him. "Christ man, you killed your sister by your neglect. What were you thinking leaving a candle burning in the kitchen? There were so many things in there that would catch that it's small wonder that anyone got out of the house. Then when your family, rightfully so, refused to help you when they found out, you killed them as well. You're the monster in this. And always have been."

"No. The fire started in the top of the house. I saw it with my own eyes." The man said that it had burned that far up before being noticed. "No. You have no idea what you're talking about."

He touched him again, and this time it was painful. When his own memories betrayed him, he sat there on the ground and thought about the candle. It had been in a bowl sitting upon the table. Wilson had put it there to show the way when he returned. Which he was never able to do. Looking up at the two men, he could see their pity and scorn. Standing up, he called for Brynhilde.

Pain shot through him. His heart, broken already, shattered into more pieces. All his pain was for naught. There had never been any fire by dragons. Not that it mattered now. They were dead, and he was alone. He realized that these people knew his secret. That they'd seen what he'd done and would tell others. His mind kept going round and round so that nothing made sense.

"We will fight until you are dead." She nodded, then bowed before him. Brynhilde didn't speak, and he wondered if she knew what he was talking about. Nothing was clear to him. "And when you are dead, I shall have peace once again. The dragons will have no choice but to do as I tell them. I still want them all dead."

"How do you suppose that's going to happen?" Wilson told Brynhilde that it would. "Just because you say so? You think that's going to work? It isn't, if you want to know the truth. There is only one ruler, one man who can command them, and that is not you."

"It will be me. I will not be made to look the fool." He thought she snorted, a very unladylike gesture, but then she'd never been a lady. "Your army? You have brought them? Not that I have any use for them, but they'll be mine as well."

"They are here." Wilson heard the buzzing before he saw them. There was an army, millions strong, and all wearing her colors. "And yours? You have brought yours as well?"

He was ashamed to call them forth. They were so few and so young that he was sure that she'd laugh at him, and that would not do. Wilson called them forward, and when their number was less than before, he looked to see them blending in with Brynhilde's. He knew they were leaving him, and not joining the other team to help him. But that was fine too. He would figure out who they were and deal with them when this was over.

"Are you ready?" She said that she was. "And you will not bow before me? You'll not allow me to take your sword?"

"Nay, I will not. I will fight you fairly, Wilson, but I will not give my sword to anyone else. Not so long as I am living."

Nodding, he moved back from her. This wouldn't be as easy as he had hoped, but soon enough he'd have the dragons dead. As soon as the men with her stepped away from him, he watched in horror as they shifted. Christ, they were all dragons.

~~~

Bryn hated that it had come to this. Before meeting the Benson family, she might have just cut his head from his shoulders and been done with it, but now she wanted to give him a chance. Let him walk away from this all with not just his head, but his dignity as well. But as soon as his men, the few that he'd brought to the line with him, reached them, she let her own men fly free. His seconds lay in tattered clothing and blood in seconds. It was never a fight, but a slaughter.

"You have defeated them all. This is not the way that I wanted this to end. You're supposed to be the one that is lying before me, begging me for your life. You have not played fairly this day, Brynhilde. And when this is over, I shall tell all who will listen that you have cheated me." Saying nothing to Wilson, she watched as the fallen bodies were taken away. They'd be buried, as was their tradition, their forms giving back to the earth that had produced them. Wilson laughed, sounding slightly insane. "I shall enjoy this."

He attacked her with magic. Bryn had no trouble moving from the arc of magic that came toward her. It was weak and without substance. Like the man wielding it, it was erratic and lackluster.

As he began to wear his magic down, she used her sword to deflect it all from her and the family. Finally, when he was spent, his body worn down from what he'd done, she stood over him with her sword at her side.

"Make it quick." She nodded and waited for him to give her the victory. "I will not concede that you won. You have cheated me out of so much by being free. That man should be killed for what he has done. You have not won fairly. You have cheated me."

"That's the way it goes sometime." She lifted her sword well above her head. It would be a quick death for him, and she looked down at him as he stretched out his neck for her. "You were a good adversary, Wilson, but this war was lost before it began."

The blade came down quickly and strongly, the swing of her blade true and magical. She heard it hit bone, knew that she'd taken his head from his shoulders with one swipe of it. Stepping back from his body, she watched his neck separate from his shoulders and his head roll forward.

His head didn't look up at her, but lay face down in the dirt. She could see the poison of his blood staining the grass, and knew that a great deal of black magic had been spent in making this man what he was. As his blackness boiled into the ground, Akassa came to stand beside her and asked her to step back. He would gladly take care that no one would know that anything happened here today, and that the earth would not remain scarred forever.

His flame burnt the ground deep. The roots would have a better chance at surviving if he killed the evilness that was spilled there. She knew that a faerie ring would be planted for the warriors that had given their lives, but nothing would be said or done for Wilson. He was gone, and the world was a better place for it. The army he had, they were following orders; this was of no fault to them.

Men that had been a part of Wilson's group came from

the woods. She did nothing more than watch them. If they wanted a fight, then they'd have it. The call to arms was met with a call to her own men, and in seconds they were ready. This fight was bloody and swift…her faeries made short work of the men there. In seconds, the hundred or so men that had wished to kill all dragons were as dead as their leader. Bryn hadn't had the need to even lift her sword; her men, all of them, had done it for the Bensons. As it should have been.

The walk back to the house was made in silence. Not only did she not speak, but the babes that had been brought and left in the back of the stand of dragons never whimpered either. The thought was to keep them safe, in the event that Wilson had men to spare and would come to the castle. She'd never seen such a pitiful group as his army had been.

"So many died today." Bryn nodded at Jacob. "Useless loss of life, if you ask me. And for what? No other reason than to come together. I don't think I like people any more than I did when the first castle was taken."

"It's not the first castle. I mean, the one that Anthony lived in, it's not the first one. There was one other." Jacob asked her how she knew. "I was there. When it was built. It was small, of course, and had fewer people in it, but it was almost in the same place as this one."

"And the king that lived there, was he a bad man?" She shrugged and said she didn't think he was. "And then Anthony came along and made all our lives better. Too bad that he was murdered like he was. He was a good man."

"He was. But the king before him, he wasn't ruthless. I mean, he had some good qualities about him." She grinned. "I think you know him."

"Nay, I'd not know him. The king Anthony, he was the

only king that I knew. He was a good one, like I said, but I wasn't around for the other man." She looked up and he did too. "Elbert know him?"

"It was Elbert. He and his wife were king and queen before Anthony came along. He was a good man, but not very good with people. Isn't that right, Elbert?" Jacob stopped walking, and she did as well, when Elbert turned to look at them. "You stepped down when a better man came along, or so I was told. I'm not so sure. Had you baked for any man or woman that came along, I think you would have won a great many wars."

"I was having my own set of troubles, my lady. And being king did not suit me as well as I would have liked." Elbert moved on, his voice carrying back to them. "My wife did take on so when I stepped down, but I had me a child to raise up to be the mother of the future king. I had the best of both worlds if you ask me."

As he moved into the castle to get things moving for dinner, Jacob turned and looked at her. He had such a comical look on his face that she couldn't help but laugh. He asked her if she was joking an old man.

"Have you ever known Elbert to joke about anything?" He looked at the castle, then back at her before shaking his head. "He was a good king, as I said, but not very good at it. It would have been only a matter of time before he was killed for what he did. And when Anthony came along and offered him a job, he took it without any hesitation. His wife, as he said, was not happy. I think she made his life more than a little miserable for a great many years before she passed in her sleep."

"In her sleep, did she?" Bryn would tell him if he asked,

but he only shook his head. "I'm thinking that I won't want to upset you much. You have a streak in you that might make me live a lot longer and healthier should I not."

"You'll be fine, Jacob, I promise you. I love you." He nodded, but looked skeptical. "I tell you what...when the time comes that we're going to have to fight, I will do so with my hands tied behind my back. That should give you an advantage, don't you think?"

"I don't know about that. I've seen your army. They'd cut me to ribbons." She laughed with him. "I know what you can do for me. You have me an armload or two of grandchildren. That would make me the happiest man on earth, at least in my little corner of it, anyway."

"Deal." He looked like he didn't believe her, and she leaned to him and kissed his weathered cheek. "I've already started on one for you."

He was still standing there with his mouth open when she walked away. She was going to have a child, one so much like her that she could no longer call herself the last of the warrior faeries. She didn't fear for this child, knowing that living here, growing up here, would keep her safe from being called upon, but she would be someone to reckon with. Forever.

Later that night she was near the water when her mates joined her. Dinner had been long finished, and the rest of the people had gone to their homes. The castle was well guarded, and everyone inside was as safe as they had been in their mothers' wombs. Leaning back on Akassa, she looked up at the moon that had been bright enough for her to see by for hours.

"I've had a long conversation with Caroline about your pregnancy. I had no idea that you would breed for so short a time." Bryn nodded, feeling the babe moving around a little. "In four months, we'll be parents. I just can't believe it."

"I can only have a child every fifth year. She told you that?" Simeon nodded. "Also, I will only have one son. He will be born second. All faerie warriors have a single male child. I'm not sure why, but that's the way it works."

"She said that there are a great many children out there after today that have no parent. I was thinking that we'd try and help them out." She looked up at Akassa as he smiled down at her. "There are also a lot of parents that have no children, and this would help them as well. I think it would do us good to match them up to some of those families. What do you think?"

"I think that's a wonderful idea, but not just any family can have one of these special children. They must be checked out. We do not want monsters taking children and harming them." He told her that he'd have it no other way. "Good, then I agree."

"The fight today, you and Tinsel, you had it worked out so that few died, didn't you?" She said that the list that they'd found in Wilson's head had helped. "But you were ready for anything. I'm very proud of you, Bryn. Very proud indeed. What can we do to help out the other families? Your army lost some as well, didn't they?"

"Tinsel is taking the names of the dead. There will be a faerie circle made in their honor. They shouldn't have been made to fight in such a war." They both agreed with her. "Also, the men who joined our group today, they will be trained to fight like our army, and their families will be taken care of. It's the way we do things. They will be paid too; some of them only took this job with Wilson because they needed the income. He didn't tell them that they may well die. It's sad really, that so many people will do just about anything for a meal, don't you think?"

She didn't say anything else, but let them talk. Bryn had a lot on her mind. Like what was she going to do now that she had no one to claim her? She looked up at Akassa when he said her name. Bryn smiled when he did.

"What would you think of seeing the world with us?" Bryn asked him what he meant. "We could travel, the three of us. And see what is out there and how much it's changed. Also, I would like to take a cruise. I've never done that. Not even with Simeon."

"You mean on a boat?" He said that was usually the mode of transportation on a cruise. "What I meant was, leaving our fate to others? I mean, I don't know about you, but my faith in humankind is a little off. Have you seen what they do to each other?"

Simeon laughed, and she asked him what was so funny. "You. I mean, you're an immortal and you're worried about a ship out to sea? Come on, it'll be fun. And maybe while we're gone we can get an early start on baby items, and Christmas is only a few short eight months away. We would be able to get some really great gifts for everyone. Besides, I promise you, if the ship sinks, I'll take you to safety first and go back for Akassa."

It was settled, sort of. They would leave next week after closing up the house and packing. Asher knew, of course, as did the rest of the family, but she was the one that would have to tell Tinsel.

Bryn knew that he'd be pleased for her, to be going on such a grand adventure, but she had to also tell him that he was going as well. There was no way she was going to leave him behind again. Bryn had missed her companion and wouldn't leave him again.

That night, while sleeping between the men in her life, she felt the presence of someone powerful. She didn't wake, but waited for the being to appear before her. For some reason, seeing Eve there didn't surprise her as much as she thought it would have.

Hello, my child. How are you enjoying being in love? She told her that it was perfect. *Yes, I know that feeling quite well. I have come to talk to you about a few things, if you do not mind.*

Never for you, my lady. Never. The place where she was standing changed. It was the castle of old, the throne room from so many centuries ago. Sitting in the seat across from the queen, Bryn had a chance to look around. *This room is a perfect match to the one that they're living in now. I'm sure you had a hand in that. I'm betting that should we walk the halls and the levels, it would be a perfect match for it.*

I only left them the tools. What they did with them was entirely up to them. She nodded. *I have made some changes for you. Being as magical as I am, it was my pleasure to do so. They are for you, for the most part, but the family as well. You will have as many children as you wish, Brynhilde. And as many sons as you can carry too. The one you carry now is a girl, as you have figured out, but the next ones will be whatever they wish to be. You are free in your sword; there is no reason that you should be dictated to on the number of children you have nor what they are. What do you think?*

Thank you. I don't know what to say. I think that is a wonderful gift that you've bestowed upon me. Eve said that she'd done enough for them all. *Speaking of the others…Asher, he came to me today. He said that the book I brought him is nonsense. You did that as well?*

Her laughter sounded like bells in a long tower, birds singing in the early spring, and water falling over a mountain all at the same time. When she took her hand in hers, it was as if she'd never died. The warmth that she gave her was felt through her body.

It was my diary as a child. I cannot imagine what Asher might think of some of the things I put to paper. And my handwriting was so poor that there were times when even I could not read it. But I needed a reason to bring you here, and that was the only thing we could think of. I do hope you'll tell him, and that you'll forgive me for such a falsehood. You were such a stubborn child, we had to give you something to do. Bryn had figured that out as well. *Are you happy, Bryn? I mean, really happy?*

Yes, as happy as I have ever been. I thank you for that, my lady. Eve nodded. *You said that you wouldn't be able to stay here, with us. Is that not true?*

Nay, it is true to a point. We cannot allow you to see us, not like before, but we shall be around. Someone needs to watch over the babes, do they not? She nodded and put her hand on her own flat belly. *You will have a dragon, Brynhilde. The only full blooded one born to this family. And he will go far in life, with the help of all the others. I'm proud to say that I never expected it, but am glad that it will be you that carries him.*

And this dragon, will he be safe? The queen nodded at her and told her that he would be very safe. *I suppose that we'll have to name him for Anthony, won't we?*

He would like that, but I have a better name for him. She nodded and asked her what it would be. After she was told, Eve started to fade. *I have to go, child. This meeting with you, it will not happen often, but there will be times when I should like to speak to someone besides the dead, and Anthony. I love him dearly, but he can be somewhat of a pain at times.*

When she woke the next morning, Bryn felt refreshed. She decided not to tell the men that she'd spoken to the queen, nor would she tell them of the children that would be born to them. There was time enough for that. They were going sailing or whatever it was called, and she was looking forward to it. But soon, she knew, she'd tell them. Maybe. To have as many children as they wished, it would be a wonderful thing to them all.

Chapter 10

Huston waited for his boss to come back and talk to him for hours. Roger was supposed to meet him here, then take him to a meeting, but he'd already decided that he wasn't going to do this. Dragons had flames. And as much as he wanted—no, needed—the money, there wasn't enough money in the world to bring him back from being a crispy critter from a dragon.

The dishes were all done; even the pots and pans were finished up and put away. But here he sat, with his thumb up his ass like he was waiting for some sort of magic to tell him what was going on. If he was honest, he didn't want to go home. Not ever again. Lately he'd been staying in the alley behind this place, trying his best to be warm and not think about his dad. The fucking bastard had hit him for the last time.

Huston was ready to call it quits when a woman appeared in front of him suddenly and he staggered back from her. She was beautiful, yeah, but she looked deadly too. There was a memory there, about her, but he tugged at it too hard and he lost it.

"Hello." He nodded. "You know me, Huston. You tried to claim me once not long ago. I'm the warrior that you thought to have all kinds of sex with. And you wanted me to kill the dragons. I told you I couldn't, remember?"

"No. I didn't want to have sex with you." His face heated up when she only looked at him. "What are you doing here anyway? I thought that you'd be out killing dragons or something. Ain't that what you were hired to do? Roger said that he was going to hire you out or something. Even that guy he told me about...Basketball or something was his name."

"His name was Wilson, and he and Roger are both dead. I told them it would happen, but they didn't want to listen. I've come to talk to you about a few things." Huston had thought that was what might have happened, but only sat down when she asked him to. "So are a great many other people that decided to end all dragons. They thought to rule the dragons too, as you and your father did, but that didn't work out so well for them."

"My dad, he's got a burr up his ass about a lot of things lately. Like the money that I had. He took most of it, and now I'm waiting on some more." He had a thought. "If what you're saying is true, there won't be any more money for me, will there? Not that I was going to take much more of it, just enough to get away. But I wasn't going to be a part of their group. I had enough of doing stupid shit and people making fun of me."

"No, that ship has sailed, as they say." He nodded, mourning the loss of it as if it were his leg. "But you need a job and I'm here to offer you one. If you can promise me a few things first. Things that I'll be watching over about you, making sure that you uphold your end of it. And if you fuck up, I'll dispatch you to hell."

She said it calmly and without threat. Her voice was all soft and stuff, but he believed her. It was there, like a bow on top of a present that you knew you wanted. He wanted a job. One that paid well and didn't have strings attached to it. Like that other thing, with Roger. He'd figured out that being around a bunch of pissed off dragons wasn't going to be healthy. To him or a lot of other people, like she'd told him.

"What kind of job?" She nodded and told him that he had one here. "Yeah, in case you didn't notice, I have that one. Washing dishes every day for some other people ain't really all that glamorous, nor does it pay well. Besides, if Roger ain't here, who the hell is going to pay me anyway? Money just don't fall in my lap. And I'm not going to steal it."

"I meant that you'd own this place, run it as you see fit. Hire people to do this job as well as others." He looked around at the place and shook his head. It was a dump. "You want something else?"

"No, I like this place well enough, but it ain't really the Ritz, now is it? I'm not saying I want to run that place either, but I think that this one is going to catch fire one night and burn to the ground without much in the way of the fire department coming out to blow it out." She looked around when he did. "I want a job. And I sort of like the idea of having a restaurant, but not here. This place isn't going nowhere. I want to be able to have money for food and a place to stay. A car in the winter months so I don't have to walk. I'm not asking for a great deal here, just some things that I've been without. I'm not asking you to give me those things, but I was just sitting here thinking about how much I'd like to be my own man and not have my dad hanging around my neck like a chain. Okay?"

"Yes, I see what you mean. There isn't much in the way of style about the place. And I don't blame you for looking out for yourself, Huston. I think you can do whatever you set your mind to." She looked at him. "I can do all kinds of things for you, Huston. Make this place nicer and cleaner, but I will expect something in return."

"Ain't that always the way? I don't have nothing for you to take. My name is worthless. I have a prison record, and no education to speak of. I can read all right, and I can figure things well when I need to. But if you tell me what you want, I'll try and do it for you. I need…I was going to say I need money, but it ain't that. I need a life." She nodded at him again. "What do you want in return for letting me running this little place? I'll have to think on it real hard, but I'd do almost anything you want within reason. I'm not going to kill anybody either. You got rules about it? Well, so do I."

"I need for you to hire some people that need a job, as you did when you started here. Give them a chance, like the one you never got by working here. Treat them better than your dad did you when you got home. Give other people, other convicts, a hand up. And a handshake." He nodded. Roger had given him a break when nobody else would, but he still turned out to be something of a dick. "And I need for you to quit your father. Let him hang himself, so to speak. Mostly, I'll take care of him if you would allow it."

"He's pissed off with me about the money. I had me a thousand dollars that I was keeping, and he found it and spent it all before I got a chance to use it to find myself a place to live. Now we're stealing again, and I just…. It's not what I want to do now. Understand?" She said that she understood more than he could know. "I can do what you want, lady, but you have to know I don't have the funds nor the knowhow to make it work. I'm not too stupid, but I don't know anything about this shit."

The little person appeared before he could stand. Huston was going to leave, make things happen for himself, even if it meant going back to prison. At least there he got three meals a day and a warm blanket. His dad even took that from him.

"This is Gardena. She will help you find your way, and keep you from making big mistakes. Her former master was a professor at the college, and he taught all kinds of classes that she learned from. She is a faerie, like me." The little woman bowed before him. "She now belongs to you, if you think you can make this work. And I have to warn you, Huston, not listening to her will be painful for you."

She stuck him in the hand with a tiny little sword. He cried out and stuck his finger in his mouth to suck the blood off it. When she sat down, he looked at her and wondered why she'd done that to him.

"We can speak now." He told her they were talking just fine before. *No, I mean in secret. Others will not always be accepting to having me at your ear. This way we can talk when we need to. And I shall do you more harm if you do not heed my words. You can make this work, Huston. I know this.*

Huston understood now and thought that with help, he might be able to make himself a living. But there was still the restaurant and how bad it was. Almost as soon as the thought entered his head, he looked around as magic — he knew that was what it was — started to make the place not just cleaner, but bigger too.

When it was done, he stood up. Careful of where he stepped, fearful that it would all go away, he turned and looked at the warrior. She told him her name and he nodded before speaking.

The appliances were brand new, and not stained or taped together. The grease in the fryer was clean; he could see himself in it. Dishes that had been chipped in so many places it was difficult to carry food in them, or to put them away, were brand new, with a large H in the middle of them. Silverware shone in the containers. There was even supplies, napkins and toilet paper, with cleaning shit too.

"You did this for me. I know you want me to hire some people like me, but there's more to it than that, huh? You need something else from me. I told you before, I don't have shit. And I don't know that I ever will." She told him he'd have whatever he wished now, but he had to work at it. "Just like that?"

"Yes, just like that. You're your own man, Huston. Don't fuck this up." He nodded. "There will be money in your account, with your name on it, only once a month. That is for you. The restaurant will also have an account with money in it, so long as you do as you've promised me. You'll see that you'll need it less and less as you succeed, but it will still be there, for you to help anyone you wish."

"And my dad? He won't be able to get to it, none of it?" She told him that Harrison would only be able to get to it if Huston allowed it. "I won't. He'd suck me dry if he was to."

After Bryn left him, Huston walked around the place again. Everything was nice. There were good benches in the dining area. New coffee machines, and a pop machine too. Even the floors, which had seen better days, looked nice and new. And all the while Gardena was with him. He sat down and asked if he could talk to her.

"Of course you can. About anything and everything. What would you like to know?" He didn't want to offend her, so he had to pause in thinking how to ask her. "I can make sure you're fed right now, should you wish. But only when we are alone."

"All right." The hot roast beef dinner appeared before him. "This is my favorite meal. My mom used to make it when there was meat enough for it. And I love mashed potatoes too. Lookee, hot rolls too. Are you being punished?"

He hadn't meant to blurt it out like that, but he'd said it and now he wanted to know. She asked him what he meant and he explained it to her. How working with him was her punishment for doing something wrong.

"Nay, I volunteered for this job with you. There were many that wanted to come here and help, but my lady said I'd be best suited to help you." He asked her if she was kidding. "No. I want to help you. And in turn, help me. I wish to be the envy of all who know me. Not nice, I know, but to make you successful will make me happy too. We will work well together, do you think?"

"Yes, but I don't know much about cooking and such." She said that she'd help him find someone. "I don't know much about ordering and things like that either. I'm just a dishwasher."

"You will be fine. The two of us will take our time and get it right. Hiring people will be simple and easy, as I can read minds. Not yours, because I belong to you, but we will be fine, I promise."

For the first time in his life, Huston thought that he might be okay. He was worried about his dad coming along and messing it up, but he was going to find him a nice place to live and stay away from him. There wasn't any point in making things bad for himself when he had it so good now. Yes, Huston was going to make this work.

~~~

Her next visit was to Harrison. He wasn't going to be as easy to fix, if she could fix him at all. Huston had wanted to change his life around, needed to, but his father was going to be a lot harder. If she could change him at all she had a feeling that it wouldn't last long. That he'd be back to his old ways in no time, and trying to bring his son along with him.

Bryn found him in the kitchen of his house. It was in ill repair; the lawn was mostly scrub and there was trash everywhere. He was trying to cook him some dinner…dinner that he'd bought himself with the stolen money from his son. Bryn let out a long breath before entering the house, just to calm her beast. Clearing her throat, she stood firm when he turned to look at her.

"Who are you? You know what, I don't care. Get out of my house. And if you're from those people that are on that committee or whatever, you can tell them for me that I'm not going to do squat until I want to." He sat down to his dinner of burnt steak and a half-done potato. She sat across from him. "Did you hear me? Get on away from here."

"I've just come from visiting your son, Huston." He called him an ungrateful cur and cut into his meat. "He's going to run the local restaurant and hire some people to work for him and with him."

"Yeah? Well, he's too stupid for that. I'll have to help him. You might want to keep that in mind when you visit him

170

again. Where's he getting the cash for that?" She told him that she'd given it to him. "Well, ain't you the nicest thing. Stupid too. Next time you're parting with money, you can give some of it to me. Like I said, I'll have to help him. That is until I get this other project going that I'm working on."

"You mean capturing a dragon? That's not going to happen. You're not going to be able to collect on that ever." He asked her why not. "Because I'm protecting them. With my life, should the need arise, but it won't. I'm an immortal, unlike you."

"You don't say." He ate another bite of his food before pushing it away. "Nobody around here to cook for me, so I have to make due. I don't suppose I can persuade you to cook me a nice fine meal, can I?"

"No, you can't. I'm here to warn you away from Huston. He's going to make something of his life, and he'll do much better without you around." Harrison laughed and she smiled at him. "If you don't do as I tell you, I'm going to kill you."

"I don't think so. First of all, you might want to think about what the police will say when they find your prints all over the house." She told him that she'd not touched anything. "Then you got your DNA shit everywhere. They'll put you in prison for the rest of your days. I ain't worth it."

"No, you're not. But back to your son. He needs for you to leave him alone." Harrison started shaking his head even before she was finished. "Why not? Don't you want him to succeed? To make something of his life?"

"I don't care if he does or not, but he's gotta take care of his old man. What sort of son would he be if he didn't?" Bryn told him a smarter man. "Now you've gone and hurt my feelings. Huston is as dumb as a rock. And he'll need me to keep him on the straight and narrow, so to speak. And that will cost you. You do want to pay me for keeping him in the flush for you, don't you?"

"No, I'm not paying you a penny." He seemed so confident in her paying him that he started listing what he was going to need in the way of cash and merchandise. "You're not going to get any of that, Harrison. Either promise me that you'll leave him alone, or you'll end up at the wrong end of death."

"This is how it's going to be. And so you know, I'm gonna get me a dragon. Have you seen how much they're worth? Christ, I'll be as rich as Simon." While she didn't know who that was, she did understand his greed. "Anyways, I'm going to mosey on over there now and prove to you that I'm going to be taking over. At least the finance part of your relationship with him."

Bryn had tried. And she didn't want to have to fuck with him anymore. Snapping her fingers, a feast appeared before the man and he looked at it greedily. She stood up and moved to the door, making sure that his greed was just a little more than it was. Not enough to kill him—she'd leave that up to him—but enough that he'd be so hungry he'd not think about the consequences of eating too quickly. Just as she was leaving, she heard him coughing. Smiling, she willed herself back to the house.

"Have you done it? Are you satisfied with the results?" She told Asher that she'd helped Huston. "And his father, he's finished as well? I know you told me that he'd be trouble, but I hope you did try."

"I did. And he won't be any more trouble to anyone after today." He eyed her and she smiled at him. "You told me that I had to make this work for the boy. I did. And the father, no matter how much faith you had in me making him understand, didn't work. He's choking on his last meal. Fitting, I think. He stole the money from Huston when that was all he had."

"I see." He didn't, but she didn't care. Rubbing her belly, she sat down when he spoke again. "The restaurant, it'll do well, you think?"

"Yes, very well. And he'll succeed with the help that we've set up for him." Bryn wanted to take a nap. Her body was exhausted from holding her form, and she felt her eyes getting heavier with each passing moment. "I have one more project to do, and after that, I'm going to sleep for a month. I have to take care of the monument to the fallen in a couple of days."

"All right. Why don't you take a nap now?" She nodded, her body sliding into sleep even as she sat there. "Simeon and Akassa are here to take you home. You need to rest more."

"I will." Arms lifted her up, and she looked into the face of the man that she loved...one of them, anyway. "I love you, Akassa. So much."

"And I you, mother of my child. Come now, off to bed with you." Nodding, she felt hands undress her. Even in her advanced state of pregnancy, they seemed to find her nakedness appealing. "Goodnight, my love."

She was closing her eyes even as blankets were pulled up over her. Exhaustion like this was too hard to fight, and she didn't. Bryn put her hand over her baby and let sleep take her.

Epilogue

Anthony watched the couple. He was going to be in so much trouble if Eve didn't make it before the big event. As he looked around for her, hoping she'd make it, he wondered where all the years had gone. And now they were here for this great day.

"I'm here." Anthony held her to him. "I was trying to stay hidden away as long as I could so that I'd not miss anything."

"As have I. But today, this minute, it's happening." They moved to the room where everyone was gathered. "Asher has things under control, as usual. I could not have asked for a better replacement than him. I swear—"

"Anthony, do hush. I want to hear what is being said." He nodded, loving his wife more today than he did even an hour ago. "They're saying soon."

"Yes, I heard that as well. Did you have any idea this was going to be today?" He knew that Eve had known about this day for many years. Her ability to see into the future was better than his. "Eve, darling, I love you."

"And I you. But no, I did not know about this. This was a surprise for even me." He nodded. She would never lie to him. "I am so excited, Anthony. Our hundredth baby is being born today, and we're here."

"We are here for every birth, my love." She kissed him on the cheek as they waited with the family. He missed them.

Over the years, it had become harder and harder for them to be with them, and not be where they could see and speak to them. They could see each of the children of their children, but they could no longer interact with them. He wanted to touch them, hold them in his arms. He'd done it once, held one of his grandchildren, but now...well, it wasn't nearly enough. As they walked the halls, seeing people that they'd not in many years, he thought of the first time he'd come to this place and the people here.

Jacob's mother had welcomed them first. It was why he'd taken such a shine to the younger man. Bethy had baked them pies too, to welcome them. She'd even invited them to dinner a few times. But she never once ate with them at the castle. It was unfitting, she told them.

Eve had befriended a lot of the families, a great many more than he could have. For some reason, they thought that he was too above them. It wasn't until Eve had started taking him along with her that he was more accepted. He loved that about his Eve. She could make a friend of anyone.

And all of it had been for naught when a man decided that they were to pay for deaths that neither of them had had anything to do with. He tried hard not to think on such things, but it was hard, especially today, on this day of happiness and love.

Anthony paused in a hallway just beyond the nurses'

station. There was a young woman there, someone that he'd seen before but not recently, who was staring at him as if she could see him. Anthony looked behind him, just to make sure that he wasn't mistaken. But there wasn't anyone there. When she approached him, pointing to a room to his left, he followed.

"Hello." He nodded at her. "I know you. I mean, I've seen images of you. You're the king of dragons. Or you used to be, correct?"

Anthony nodded and held onto his mate when she joined them. The young woman knew her as well, and he felt uncomfortable. He wasn't sure what was going on, but he didn't like it. Not one bit.

"Who are you? You look like someone that we should know." She nodded at them. "How is it that you're seeing us?"

"My great grandmother is Lindsey. She speaks with the dragons. When I was born, it was said that the moon was full and that the storm came in so violently that I was named for it. My name is Storm." Anthony remembered that night too. It was a good, long time ago, but he remembered it. "And as for how I can see you, I've always been able to. I'm sort of an odd duck out when it comes to magic, like my mom before me. She so loves you guys; did you know that?"

"I think her brilliant. But what do you mean, odd duck? In what way?" Storm didn't answer them, but looked to their right. The woman standing there was a nurse, and she asked Storm what she needed.

"Nothing. Just waiting for the baby to come. You can go now, and not bother us again, please. And thank you for your services. You're a good person." The nurse looked confused, but left without another word. "I can manipulate people into doing things I want. Well, sort of what I want. Like just now, that's easy, but I have other talents as well. I can see the dead, talk to them, help them. I love that part of my magic. Do you need help?"

"No." He wasn't sure why he was so set against her helping them, but when the girl laughed, he smiled. There was something very familiar about it, like Lindsey had joined them. "We're here to see the baby born and nothing more. I don't want to take you from that. It's a big event."

"All right. My great grandmother is coming. So, you can feel better about me being here. But until she does, I'd like to talk if you don't mind." She sat on the bed and smiled at them. "When you were killed all those decades ago, it was violent. The kinsmen that were with you tried to help, but they couldn't do much against so many. You were brilliant in making sure that your children were safe, and in that, you helped a great many people, not just your family, but many."

"We were only worried for the hatchlings and a few other people. We would like to have saved them all, but it would have been impossible." Storm nodded at Eve. "When I was killed, I had hidden myself away so that I could take care that our children and those born to protect them were safe as well. It was purely a selfish act, I'm afraid. You make it sound as if we were heroic, when all we wanted to do was keep them safe. It's all we ever wanted."

"Not to the others that you saved." The door opened and Lindsey walked in. She looked just as she had all those years ago when they first saw her as a new mate to Jed and Zac. "My great grandmother is the only one that knows what sort of powers I hold. And the only reason that she does is because, as I said, I'm odd duck out."

"I don't understand what that means." Storm told Lindsey that they were there and what they wanted to know. Lindsey laughed, her beautiful voice making him smile again. "What does it mean, you're odd duck out?"

"She's different than the rest in her magic. Not as powerful as Lelani, nor as elemental, but she is as strong as Essie is in some things. It's as if she got a bit of everyone mixed into her body. She is very powerful, especially with being able to work with the passed on." Lindsey held Storm's hand as she continued. "I've been helping her when I can. Mostly it is to lend her some of my magic, but today, we had hopes that you'd be here and that we could talk."

"I want to help you." Eve asked in what way. "To bring you back to us. I've been working with a couple of people, using their magic to bring them here. I would very much like to have you join us. Would you like that? To be among us again? I know that I would, as would a great many people."

"You mean as ghosts that can be seen?" Storm shook her head at him. "Oh. Then I don't understand. What can you do for us?"

She smiled again, and he was struck by how much she looked like Lindsey. His son too, he supposed, in a female sort of way. But when she laughed, which she did often, he knew that was purely the woman with her, their Lindsey. He'd forgotten what was being said for a moment, and asked her what she meant.

"I'd like to bring you here, as Grandpa and Grandma Benson are. To be whole." Anthony staggered back; he wasn't going to get his hopes up on something like this if it was a joke. When she stood up, Storm came toward them, but slowly, as if she were afraid of startling them. "You see, as I was saying, when you were killed, it was violent. And the magic that does this has rules about that. Vengeance, mostly. They don't want the dead who have been murdered or killed in such a way to be able to return and harm those, or the family of those, that brought them to their deaths. But with you, you did so much to insure that your family would be safe. Making arrangements that babies be born with more than they might have had. Some of them even brought into the world when their fate was sealed that they would not. And through this all, you could have left here. Left the kingdom and started anew. That, my dear grandparents, is the most unselfish act there is. And that negates all the things before, all the thoughts of vengeance that you might have. It's not in your hearts any more than it was back then."

"I don't understand." It wasn't as if he didn't understand, but he didn't want to believe. She seemed to have understood that and nodded at him. "We've been gone for so long. In fact, we were just speaking that we'd not return. It's hard on us, being here but not."

"We would miss you. And even though they can't see you, they know that you're around. I've let them know." Eve asked how it would work, if it would work. "Yes, it'll work. It will drain us all for a little while. So, I'd very much like to wait until the baby is born. That way, Shelby will have all she needs for her child. But after, as soon as she's asleep, I'd like to do this for you. I need to do this for all of us. We all, as a family, need you here with us. And the babies, those here and coming, they would so love to see their grandparents. You both."

"You're saying that it does work." Storm told him it

did work, but she'd never brought a dragon back. "You're thinking that there is a chance that we might not come back at all."

"No. I'm saying that you might not be a dragon when I bring you back. I can do it, it's just a matter of your other halves." He wanted to tell her that he needed his dragon, but thought about seeing the children of his children, all of them that he'd not been able to before. "As I said, that part I'm unsure of."

"Do it." He looked at Eve when she spoke. "Anthony, to hold our babies. To be able to hug them. Tell them to their faces how much we love them. Don't you think it would be worth it to not be a dragon? I do. I'd give almost anything to see them, to touch them. And to read them a story at night? That would be the most wonderful gift of all."

"Whatever you wish, my love. You know that I want whatever you do, but I cannot help but be a little fearful of this. I mean, without our dragons, what will we be?" And he did. In that moment, he really did want her to be happy. She told him that was what she wanted, for them to be happy again. "We'll wait, as she said, and then we'll see them."

"Whatever you wish, child, it's yours. I swear to you. Even should this not work at all, I am so grateful that you thought of us, of bringing us to the family. You have no idea how much we have missed them. And seeing them every day." Storm laughed, as did Lindsey. "You only have to ask, I'll get it for you."

"You've given me life. You might not have been the one that birthed me, but you made it possible for me to have a life. A husband that I love. Children that mean the world to me. And an ability to help those, like yourself, that need me." Storm looked at Lindsey and smiled. "And you made it possible for me to have the most amazing parents and grandparents that a woman could hope for. For that, I'd do anything that you wanted."

Anthony watched the family when Storm left them to be with them. They followed, but at a slower pace. He wanted to be a part of it now, to be there while they waited, and he would be, soon, he hoped. As the day wore on, so did his excitement. He'd be there soon, he hoped.

~~~

Asher and the others formed a circle around the couple. He knew that they were there in form, but for now all he could see were the bodies that had been wrapped in the finest silk they could find, so lovingly, over the years.

Each year since the castle was finished, they'd come here and had a nice celebration. Just him and his brothers would circle around the couple that had saved them from certain death, and each of them would tell of their year. What children had been born to them, what kind of advancements had come about, and of the life in the town that they helped keep going. But this visit was going to be different.

Storm had come to him several weeks ago, telling him what she could do and what she wanted to try. He knew, like the rest, that she was very talented, that she could and did help with those that had passed over. But when she asked about the dragon king and queen, her grandparents too, he'd told her all he knew then given her a book. One that was written by them all on the things they'd found and heard about the night they had been killed. After that, she said she was going to bring them to the family.

"All right. Just hold hands with the person next to you,

and once I start, you'll begin to feel the drain." Each of them nodded, and Kiaran asked if they'd be better as dragons. "Yes, that would be better. I know that he's stronger than you are as a human."

The shift was done quickly and they all stood together. Man to dragon, and around they went. Twelve of them, ready to begin. Asher felt the first touch of magic as Storm began to work it. He had to let out a long breath to calm his nerves.

To have them here would be perfect, he knew. They had been a big part of their lives even before today. Each of them would speak to them, call on them for strength. And even the dragons had continued to name their children for them. There was one dragon, Silco, who had one child named for each letter in Anthony's name. Asher wondered if he had any more that he'd named for Eve. Smiling, he thought of the small dragons.

There were so many of them now, all breeding like they hadn't in a great many years. And when they passed from this world to the next, giving themselves to the earth and air, a faerie ring would be placed in their honor, and then a marker, so that any who passed that way would know that a great magical creature had been on this earth. Asher couldn't pass one, even if the dragon had been gone a great many years, without stopping and speaking to them, telling them they were missed.

The children of his brothers, all of them, had never left the area for very long. Going away to college was about as far as they went. Some of them bringing home brides, others just showing up, as if they'd been called here by something special. He was sure that was the way it should have been too.

Asher supposed, in a way, they all had been called here.

Even himself. Long ago he'd come here with a mission in mind, and had found love. A love so deep and strong that he doubted anything would be stronger. He loved them more than he could ever explain to someone, and was just as happy as they were when they found their other halves. He thought of his own mate and how much he loved her with every beat of his heart.

Are you supposed to be paying attention? He said that he was only here for strength. *Oh. Well, we've decided that you need us as well. We're about to you. The others and me. I can't believe that anyone thought they could do this without us.*

Me either, love. Me either. Shall I tell Storm, or should I just wait for you to show up? She said she was nearly there and she'd tell her. He saw her seconds before he felt his strength waning. And before he knew it, he was on the ground looking up at her. "Hello, darling. I'm glad that you're here."

"Me too, you moron. I told you to eat before you left." Standing up with her help, he was glad to have her extra strength. When the other mates joined them, he could feel the surge of power run over them. Even Storm looked as if she felt it. In a matter of minutes, he was feeling better than he had before the women showed up.

The shadowy figures began to appear. They were holding each other, their forms beginning to take the shape of the couple that he had heard so much about. As the magic began to drain him more, he could see the face of Anthony and that of Eve. Soon, he knew they'd be whole.

"Asher?" He nodded to Anthony and smiled. "My goodness, I think it might work. I will be able to touch you all. I hope you know that after I get hugs from you all, I want a baby to hold. It's been far too long."

"Yes, sir, I hope so, too." Anthony faded then, his body becoming just a shadow. To say he was disappointed would have been a gross understatement. And when he came back to them, not as solid looking but nearly so, he held his breath and didn't speak again, fearing that's what might have done it.

It was nearly an hour before Storm stepped back. He loved this kid, and had been there for her birth. And she could banter with him as well as her grandmother could. When she staggered away, he picked her up in his arms and held her until she said she was all right. Then he held her a little while longer until he was sure. Setting her on her feet, he smiled when she asked him what had happened.

He looked back at the couple. They hadn't made it over, as far as he could tell. They were formed and he could see them, but they weren't solid. The disappointment was heavy to him as he told Storm.

"I'm so sorry." He was as well, and told her that it wasn't her fault, that he was proud that she'd tried. "I thought I could bring them. I honestly did."

"You tried, and even now we can see them." She nodded and stood up. As she made her way to the former king and queen, he held onto Essie. "She's so disappointed. I can only imagine what they're feeling."

"I know. I had such high hopes."

No one said a bad thing toward Storm. She had tried, and that was what was important. Even Anthony, his sadness almost palatable, told her that he couldn't have had a better person trying to do this for him. All in all, it was a failure, but no one was placing blame.

"I think we'll stay here tonight. I'd like to see the castle, but in the morning, when there is more light." Asher didn't point out to Anthony that it was as bright in there as it was during the day with electricity, but only nodded. "Eve is taking this very hard. As am I. So I don't think we'll be much company. We'll see everyone tomorrow."

"All right, sir. If you need anything, just give me a call. I'll come to you."

Anthony thanked him and they left. Asher felt as if he'd had a nice big gift and was told that it wasn't really his in the first place. To have them so close and then be taken away hurt him in ways he'd not expected.

Conversation was quiet, each of them dealing with their disappointment. He held Essie's hand, and Kiaran held her other one. She was crying, saying how much she had wanted it to work, but not loud enough for anyone to hear. He knew that she'd be a mess when they got home, where she could let it all go.

Asher sat in his office after they all left or had gone to bed. He was tired, but he had some things to do before he laid his head down. As he began searching for someone to touch up some old photos, Howard, the butler, came into the room with him. It was just after midnight.

"Sir there is.... I opened the door thinking it was the young man who stocks up the wood, but it wasn't. I stood there like a fool until.... Perhaps you should come with me." He stood and asked if he needed his sword. Howard burst out laughing and said no. "I don't think it would work anyway. It's not like that. No one is storming the castle, so to speak."

He picked up his gun and called out to Kiaran to meet him in the kitchen. Even as he came down the stairs as his dragon, Asher wasn't sure if that would help. Something had spooked Howard, and he wasn't one that was easily alarmed.

The kitchen lights were all on. He didn't see anything amiss until he turned to Howard. And there they stood. Anthony and Eve.

"They came to the back door because they saw the light on." Howard sat down on the seat and continued. "I was startled, as you can imagine. I've never met them before, but their paintings hang in the big room. So I knew who they were. They were just standing there, as lost as I was about how to proceed. Then the lady, she suggested that I go and get you, since she knew you to be awake. So I did."

Howard was babbling. Not that Asher blamed him…he was in a deep sort of shock as well. Handing the gun that was useless to Howard, the man stood up and said that he'd put it away now. Then he was gone.

"Hello, Asher. My goodness, it's lovely here." Kiaran shifted, his body taking his human form as he made his way to his parents. His mom smiled at him as he put out his hands to touch her. "Oh son, it's so wonderful to see you."

They hugged for ten minutes. First with all three of them, then Asher was invited. When Essie joined them, she told them how she'd told the others who was there, and they were on their way. Soon they had to move their reunion from the kitchen to the big room, or living room, to accommodate them all.

They were a family, extended back for more generations than he could ever imagine. And they were all here in the castle that had brought them all together. Asher held his children to him as they got to know grandparents, grandparents so far back that he didn't bother with the greats. They were grandparents, same as his parents. Children were brought out, all of them connected to these people. Asher had never been as proud as he was at this moment, and knew as the years went on he'd be prouder still.

Breakfast was a huge affair. No one slept that night as they visited and ate. Asher sent out for food, drinks, and wines. Even pizza, something that Eve had wanted for so long, was brought to them. It was a day that none of them would ever forget, nor would likely want to. They were together. Forever.

Anthony and Eve

Anthony had gotten in the habit of coming outside daily with his cup of tea and watching the morning doings. Today was a school day, so most of the older children were dressed and waiting to be taken to the new school.

He sat under the big oak that had been in this yard for many years, sipping the brew and smiling as they made their way around. As he sat there, one of his grandchildren, one-year-old Paige, backed her little bottom up and sat down on him. Then she leaned back and laid her small red curly head on his chest. It was like this every morning that the weather permitted it.

Eve, the love of his life, came to sit with them, her long legs spread out before her, and he smiled. Whoever had invented shorts needed to be memorialized. He thought them the sexiest thing ever invented, and loved seeing his lady wife in them. Before he could comment, she spoke quietly.

"Have you told them?" He knew what she was asking, but he played dumb, just to see her riled up. "You know very well what I'm speaking about. We leave tomorrow, and you have not let anyone know that, have you?"

"Nay. If I were to tell them we were leaving tomorrow, then they'd want to know why. I've not gotten to that point yet in wanting to share." She glared at him and he nearly laughed. But the look in her eyes warned him he might be better if he didn't. "You'd not hurt this old man with a child in his lap, would you, love?"

"Grandpa, you are vexing Grandma. Again." He looked up at little Asher when he spoke. "I come for a hug. I have to be at school all day today, and I want to be with you."

"I know, but when you return home, we'll have a great adventure." Asher smiled at him and took off for the bus, but returned quickly to hug both him and Eve. "He is going to be a good man, don't you think?"

"Yes, I do, but you didn't answer my question. Are you going to tell them that we leave on the morrow?" He didn't want to. It broke his heart to leave here. And all of this. "Anthony, they're going to find out, and when they do, it will hurt their feelings that you didn't share."

"Do you think I don't know that? I just.... This is so personal, my love. I don't want them to make jest of me." She said that they'd never do that. "But they might. And I'm not sure I could go through with the rest should they do that."

"They're in the castle right now, having a nice breakfast. They are waiting on us." He asked her if she'd set him up. "Of course I did. Had I waited on you, we'd be leaving in the morning and no one would be the wiser. Come now. Paige is going to her nanny, and you and I are going to the castle."

She handed him several books, and he didn't bother looking. He knew what they were as surely as he knew that the children loved his dragon. Smiling a little, he thought of the fun he had with them, the children and his dragon. But this had to be done, today.

The dining room was filled with his family. Sally and Jacob were seated at the long table, while his sons were on either side of their mates. It was a glorious sight, to see them all there, and know that they were as much a part of him as was the castle. They made him welcome, and he realized that Eve was leaving this to him.

"We depart tomorrow, for New York." He should have worded it better, but was too afraid of their reactions. "I've been busy, you see. And I did something that I wanted. I've not been able to do that for a long while, and I wanted to do this. It was fun. And scary. You've no idea how hard it's been just to get it finished in a timely matter. Well, it wasn't so bad—"

"Dad? What are you trying very hard not to say?" He looked at his oldest son and smiled. "Come on, have a sit with us and explain. We're here for you no matter what you had fun at."

"Yes, of course you would be." He handed around the books that Eve had given him. "I did that. The story is mine, but the drawings, your mother did those. She has a fine hand, don't you think? And she's captured the children so well. Look, there is little Asher and Tinsel."

They were so quiet that he was nervous. Each of them looked at the books he'd given them, trading them around until Asher sat his down in front of him and regarded him. Anthony felt the stare all the way to his toes. He asked him what he thought.

"You are leaving tomorrow for New York. Would you

mind telling me why? I mean, these books are wonderful, and you're right, the drawings are amazing. Why are you leaving here?" He nodded and picked up the first book in the series. "Anthony?"

"They've made the best seller list. All of them have." Asher asked him how long he'd been doing this. "Several years, I guess. I've a total of ten out now. Each of them a different adventure with the dragons and children. They meet all kinds of things along their ways. Fish and faeries. One there is a story about how nature makes the faeries that work for her."

"And you never thought to tell us?" He looked at Essie and heard the hurt in her voice. "These are the stories that you read to the children, aren't they? You bring out your own books and read them to them all."

"Yes, well, they're in them. They like to hear about themselves." He felt his face heat up when he realized that the grandchildren knew more than his own children did. "It started out as something to keep me busy. I sit with them every day, and when they are put down for their naps or go off to school, I was just sitting around waiting for them to return. One day, I started writing them down. Eve found them and drew small drawings in the margins, and we had fun with them. Then she sent them to a publishing house, without my knowledge. They not only loved them, but paid me for them."

Pulling out his wallet, a new thing for him even after all these years, he showed it to them. Asher laughed and Jacob asked him why he'd not cashed it. He didn't need the money, and the check itself meant more to him than the money would anyway.

"They wanted them all. I mean, Eve is still drawing some of the stories for me, so they'll need to wait on those. And the faeries, they've been helping with the colors that we used. Not that they use those in the big house, but it's been fun." Asher still hadn't said anything, and he was getting worried. None of the boys had said anything, as a matter of fact. "Are you vexed at me?"

"A little, yes." He felt his heart shatter at the words from his son. Casdon shook his head as he continued. "Did you think we'd not want to be proud of you? Or was there something else? I'm sorry if we've made it so that you felt like you couldn't come to us about it. This wondrous and amazing thing that you've done."

"They're about dragons." Keion said he was well aware of that. "Don't you see? I've broken the very laws that I helped make. I told others about dragons."

"You told stories to your grandchildren and wrote them down. No one, save these children, would ever believe that there are real dragons, Dad. I mean, they might want to believe, but their parents won't ever believe." He nodded, and started to argue more with Zak when he put up his hand to continue. "I don't know about the rest of them, but I think this is the most amazing thing that I've ever seen. My dad and mom wrote books."

The rest of them told him how proud they were of them. And as they drifted away to start their days, he looked at Asher. He'd been silent through the entire thing, and he so wanted him to be pleased as well. Essie and Eve left him there and he looked at his king, the man who he had known for a great many years, and asked him if he was mad.

"Not for what you've done, no. I think, like the rest of them, that you've done a great job. I love the fact that you did it. But I'm hurt that you didn't think we'd care. Because that's it, isn't it?" Anthony felt like a small child caught doing something that he wasn't supposed to. "We love you. You do know that, don't you?"

"Oh yes. What a thing to ask. Yes, I know that you love me. But I was...I was embarrassed that I did this. Not that I did the stories, but that other people seemed to enjoy them so much. And the children? My goodness, Asher, they write letters to me." Asher smiled at him and said that was wonderful. "Eve said that I should have told you from the start, but to be honest with you, I wanted this for myself for a little while. You know, it's something that I held to me for a time."

"I can understand that as well. And it makes knowing that you kept it from us a lot better." Anthony told him he was sorry. "No need to be. As I said, I understand. But I do have a question for you. Can we go with you? To New York?"

"You wish to see me on television?" Asher was shocked by that. "I might have forgotten to mention that, didn't I?"

"Yes, you did, but that's all right. We can make a time of it. The kingdom will be all right for a little while. The children have their parents. My own are too old for me to watch after. Essie and Kiaran and I, we'd love to be there. The others too, should you like."

"I'd like that very much." He stood up and noticed that all the books were in front of Asher. "You keeping those?"

"Only if you'll sign them for me."

He felt so pleased that someone had asked that he did so with a flourish. "I've been practicing my last name. It's all so new to me, this need of a surname." He wrote Anthony Dawood, then drew a small dragon under his name. "I thought that cute. And Eve, she said I have a fine hand at it too."

~~~

Eve watched her mate as he talked about the stories that he had written. It made it so much easier to have him look only at the man speaking to them rather than the cameras and such that were all around. There was so much going on too.

You are so beautiful, my love. She smiled at him as he spoke to her. *We shall celebrate tonight, all of us, that this is done.*

It is only the beginning, and you know it. The rest of the books are finished too. He asked her when she'd done that. *While you sat upon your bottom with a child upon your lap. You are the best pillow I think any of them have ever used. You know that, don't you?*

I so love them there. It is as calming as your beating heart to me. She told him she loved him. *And I you. Forevermore.*

They had been to New York before, of course, though not for a great many decades. When they'd been here, there had been no large buildings that blocked out the sky, nor were there as many people. And the number of cars made her want to rush back home to their little spot and hide away. But there were the shops now that she was enjoying.

Last night when they'd arrived, she and the girls, with Sally, had gone shopping. She'd never been to so many stores that carried clothing. And the shoes. She had bought herself six pairs of them, and several more shorts. And the little two piece bathing suit she was saving for when they returned home. She thought that Anthony would enjoy it most of all.

They had also done some shopping for the children. There were so many of them now, too many to count, but she loved each and every one of them. And buying for them was such a pleasure for her. But sitting here, with her mate and one true love, was the greatest joy she had.

They had written so many books, some that the children

would never know of. Eve had told tales about their adventures as dragons, but adult versions. That was fun for them, writing out sex scenes and then having fun trying them out. Some of them were as outlandish as the children's stories, but no less successful.

As the television show wrapped up, Eve stretched a little, careful of the things that had been attached to her dress. And when the little voice in her ear, a microphone, they'd called it, told them they were clear, she stood up and waited for someone to take them off her.

"Would you like to have lunch with me?" She stared at the young man who had pulled the microphone off her blouse, and smiled. Men were forever a mystery to her, especially humans. "I know this quaint little place that we can have a quiet afternoon. It's my place."

"I don't think so." He smiled at her, and it wasn't friendly. "I have a husband and children older than you."

"I don't care. I think you're sexy." She only huffed at him and looked for Anthony. He was with their publisher. "He'll never have to know you came with me. A man who writes children's books is probably a pervert anyway."

Her temper, something that she'd never had any trouble with before, surged forward. It was like she was hot with it. Even her dragon seemed to roar out. But the man, instead of being afraid, thought her sexier. The fool.

"Get yourself away from me, or I shall make you regret ever being born." Essie came to stand with her then, having no doubt heard her anger. "He's making some sort of proposition with me."

"He's flirting, and clumsily too." Essie stared at the man, then smiled at him. "You are not going to get away with this;

you know that, don't you?"

Anthony came to stand behind the man when he asked Essie what she was talking about. Anthony only touched the man, just put his hand on his shoulder, when he suddenly started screaming in pain. The sleeve of his jacket was on fire, small flames shooting up around his face. Anthony made a show of helping him, but all he did was fan the fire.

Eve told him enough and he stepped back, the small flames going out. The man started screaming that she'd hurt him, that she'd set him afire when she only stood there. Essie held her hand, but neither of them commented. Anthony asked if they were all right.

"Yes. He tried to get me to go with him. He said that we could have a quick lunch at his home. I told him no, but he was persistent." Mr. Calloway, the manager of the show they'd just been on, came from the group around them. Eve repeated her story to him, and he glared at the young man.

"You've been told about touching people when they tell you no." The man, Scott his name tag said now that she could see it, said that she'd set him on fire. "Yes, I'm sure she did. And she's a dragon too. Moron."

Mr. Calloway knew just what they were, and winked at her when he bent to help young Scott up and to the door, none too gently either. As soon as he was out of sight, she nearly fell into Anthony's arms.

"He won't be believed." Eve told him that she knew that. "The idiot. He's lucky that I didn't really burn him to a crisp. He should know better than to touch what is mine. Are you all right, love?"

"I am, but I'm ready to leave." He asked her to home or the hotel. "Both, but we're to have that dinner with the children, so I won't miss that. He was so...I don't know, but it made me sick the way he treated me."

"Yes, well, he'll never do that again." She asked him if he'd killed him. "No, I only took care that he cannot have an erection again. It wasn't hard. I mean, literally, he was never hard."

They were still laughing as they entered the limo. The ride to the hotel wasn't long, but it was good to get away from people for a few minutes. As her love held her, she thought of how humans were no different, not really, than they had been from her time. Only they were bolder. She didn't think she cared for that any more than she did before.

"Anthony, when we return from this, do you think we could have a nice picnic by the lake? As we used to do?" He said that he liked that idea. "Just you and I, and we'll turn off those blasted cell phones too."

"I think that is a perfect idea, my love. We'll have Elbert make us some of his scones and some tea. Those thermos things are wonderful for that sort of thing now." She agreed with him. "Then we'll take us a blanket and make love, right there on the edge of the water, and look up at the stars when we finish."

"I could never be finished with you, Anthony." He kissed her then, and she felt his hunger for her as well as his love. "You and I, we are so lucky, aren't we? We have our lives back, children galore, as well as our dragons. Who would have thought, all those years ago, that we'd come back here to watch over them all?"

"Not I, ever. When the pike pierced my heart, all I could think about was that you were gone from my life, never my heart, but my life. And that I'd miss you." She said the same feelings had come over her. "As I lay there dying, I thought of all the things we'd done, all the people that we had touched to make our children safe, and I felt at peace. For the first time in a long while, I was at peace with my life."

She lay there, his heart beating under her ear, and thought of her life thus far. They were very lucky, she thought. Not just to be here, in this time, but to have so many loved ones around them. To her, there weren't enough words, nor the right ones, to say how much it meant to her to have all that she did.

Akassa and his loves had prospered so much, more than the rest of them, she thought. He was happy too, with Simeon and Bryn by his side. With Bryn's magic they had helped so many people, children included, and that made her so proud of them all. She thought of all her children, they were the happiest of all. And they enjoyed life to the fullest too. Eve could not wait for more adventures from them to come along. Not to mention their children too.

When they were in their hotel room again, she thought of another book she wanted to write. This one, she knew, would be hers alone. It was going to be about the love affair between two dragons who would someday be king and queen of their kind. Yes, she thought, she'd write it, and she and Anthony would add to it over the years to come. A Tale of Two Dragons, that would be the name of it.

AWARD WINNING, BESTSELLING AUTHOR

Kathi Barton, winner of the Pinnacle Book Achievement award as well as a best-selling author on Amazon and All Romance books, lives in Nashport, Ohio with her husband Paul. When not creating new worlds and romance, Kathi and her husband enjoy camping and going to auctions. She can also be seen at county fairs with her husband who is an artist and potter.

Her muse, a cross between Jimmy Stewart and Hugh Jackman, brings her stories to life for her readers in a way that has them coming back time and again for more. Her favorite genre is paranormal romance with a great deal of spice. You can visit Kathi on line and drop her an email if you'd like. She loves hearing from her fans. aaronskiss@gmail.com.

Follow Kathi on her blog: http://kathisbartonauthor.blogspot.com/

www.ingramcontent.com/pod-product-compliance
Lightning Source LLC
Chambersburg PA
CBHW020623180626
46810CB00007B/2909